STUART MCHARDY is a storyteller, writer, poet, musician, broadcaster and lecturer on Scottish history and folklore. Since graduating with a history degree from Edinburgh University in the 1970s he has found ongoing inspiration and stimulus in Scotland's dynamic story and music traditions. His research has led him far beyond his native land and he has lectured and performed in many different parts of the world. Whether telling stories to children or lecturing to adults, Stuart's enthusiasm and love of his material make him an entertaining and stimulating speaker.

His own enthusiasm and commitment have led to him re-interpreting much of the history, mythology and legends of early Western Europe. Combining the roles of scholar and performer gives McHardy an unusually clear insight into tradition and he sees connections and continuities that others may have missed. As happy singing an old ballad as analysing ancient legends, he has held such diverse positions as Director of the Scots Language Resource Centre and President of the Pictish Arts Society. He lives in Edinburgh with the lovely Sandra and they have one son, Roderick.

By the same author

Strange Secrets of Ancient Scotland (Lang Syne Publishers, 1989)

Tales of Whisky and Smuggling (Lochar, 1992)

The Wild Haggis an the Greetin-faced Nyaff (Scottish Children's Press, 1995)

Scotland: Myth, Legend and Folklore (Luath Press, 1999)

Edinburgh and Leith Pub Guide (Luath Press, 2000)

Scots Poems to be read aloud (Editor) (Luath Press, 2001)

Tales of Whisky and Smuggling (House of Lochar, 2002)

The Quest for Arthur (Luath, 2002)

The Quest for the Nine Maidens (Luath Press, 2003)

MacPherson's Rant and other tales of the Scottish Fiddle (Birlinn, 2004)

The Silver Chanter and other tales of Scottish Piping (Birlinn, 2004)

School of the Moon: the Scottish cattle raiding tradition (Birlinn, 2004)

On the Trail of Scotland's Myths and Legends (Luath Press, 2005)

The Well of the Heads and other Clan Tales (Birlinn, 2005)

Luath Storyteller: Tales of the Picts (Luath, 2005)

On the Trail of the Holy Grail (Luath, 2006)

The White Cockade and other Jacobite Tales (Birlinn, 2006)

Luath Storyteller: Tales of Edinburgh Castle (Luath, 2007)

Scotland the Brave Land

10,000 Years of Scotland in Story

STUART McHARDY

Luath Press Limited

EDINBURGH

www.luath.co.uk

First published 2012

ISBN 978-1-908373-49-6

The paper used in this book is recyclable. It is made
from low chlorine pulps produced in a low energy, low emission
manner from renewable forests.

Printed and bound by
CPI Group (UK) Ltd, Croydon, CRO 4YY

Typeset in 11 point Sabon by
3btype.com

contents

CLANS AND CULTURE

LANDSCAPE

WILD LIFE

scotland

Where Legends Come to Life

HE SUCCESS OF the animated movie 'Brave' is a bold reminder, were any needed, that Scotland is a treasure trove of myth and legend.

The oldest layers of story grow quite literally out of the landscape. They are about the gods, goddesses, giants and heroes who made our country. Whether by acts of boastfulness and bravado such as mountain tossing and rock putting, or by acts of generous love that allow rivers and springs to flow, lochs to form and the land to take life – the elemental forces are all around in wave, rock, storm and stream. Scotland is a brave land, a stronghold of the free, yet it is a stronghold that nurtures and protects her children, and welcomes the stranger. Storytelling is the hospitable art.

After the creation myths, come legends such as the Saints tales of Columba, Ninian and Mungo; sagas of Norse settlers and raiders, historical tales of the independence heroes William Wallace and Robert Bruce, and stories of the Highland and the Border clans. These flow seamlessly into later stories of inventors and explorers along with numerous pioneers in education, international friendship and human rights.

But all of these stories arise too from Scotland's diverse cultural geography. Facing outwards north, east and west

SCOTLAND THE BRAVE LAND

by sea – and south by land – Scotland is a crossroads
of people and events. Moreover, within our big small
country there are formidable barriers of mountain and
loch that divide different areas of cultural influence and
tradition. With Gaelic, Pictish, Scots, Germanic, Norse,
Flemish, Mediterranean, old British and Atlantic cultures
all lapping at our shores, and taking root in different
regions, Scots have never been wanting for choice when
it comes to songs and stories.

After these waves of myth and legend comes the
tsunami of our Scottish folk tales. Stories of the little
people, of ghosts, tricksters, derring-do lassies, wicked
magicians and magical helpers are all around us in
the landscape, often perpetuating yet older traditions.
These stories are also found in the cities where new forms
of urban community and entertainment developed from
the old. City dwellers are keen to stay connected with
the hills and valleys in which they are located.

The key thing in folktales was to entertain while also
passing on lots of cultural knowledge and life wisdom.
In our own time these folk traditions have experienced a
remarkable renaissance as new storytellers have taken up
old themes and given them back to a wider audience.
Perhaps 'Brave' itself is part of that movement of
rediscovery and reinvention.

As long as people want to tell and to enjoy stories,
then the storytelling traditions will remain alive,
continuous yet ever changing in new contexts. Scots of all
ages and cultures like to talk! The river of memory,

entertainment and wisdom is as unstoppable as the moment Auld Mither Cailleach unplugged the well of stories and let it flow.

But however excellent Scotland's storytellers, authors, poets and filmmakers may be, there is only one place to truly enjoy these traditions and that is in Scotland – where the legends were born and where their authentic life remains. When you see the land then you can recognise the stories for what they truly are – the life and soul of a whole country. Equally, without stories the land is a territory unknown, unmapped, unfriendly. We are all the children of our landscape and when we feel that kinship then the stories and the songs begin to bubble up.

The game changing ecologist Patrick Geddes, a Scotsman of the industrial age, coined the phrase 'think global, act local.' If we love our own land, tend it like a garden, and share its gifts, then the whole earth can once again flower and flourish. Brave land makes beautiful planet. Stuart McHardy has provided an ideal threshold for Scotland's older storytelling traditions. It is my pleasure to open the door and invite you inside.

Donald Smith
Director
Scottish Storytelling Centre

introduction

COTLAND HAS BEEN described as a land of
story. In fact it has been said that there is
hardly a stream or a rock that does not have
its own tale. It is true that many places have
their own tales for, like people everywhere, the
Scots have always had a deep love of the land and a great
respect for those who went before, our ancestors. In the
modern world we are dominated by the idea of history
as the written word, but for tens if not hundreds of
millennia humans only had stories to tell them who they
were and where they came from. And story survives
despite the introduction of writing, television, computer
games and increasingly sophisticated means of electronic
communication. All of them need stories. Story is in our
hearts and seems almost to be in our DNA. Children come
into the world surrounded by story and it is no accident
that what are thought of as children's stories are often
rooted in the far past and draw up on myth and legend
for their ongoing power and popularity. And in Scotland
we are blessed that the art of story-telling, whether in our
schools, our homes, or in the pub, has never gone away.
Nowadays of course we have storytelling clubs and there
have never been as many storytellers.

Scotland's tales are rich in all aspects of the human
story. This collection taken from a variety of earlier

compendia of our native tales covers the far past, our kings and castles, our deepest myths and legends, the culture of our Highland clans, our landscape and the supernatural. It tells of our beautiful landscape but also the psychological reality of who we are. We continue to tell our stories to remind us of who we are, to honour our ancestors and to help educate our children. For truly in this ancient country storytelling has never faded. And hopefully this small selection of our tales can serve as an introduction to the vast treasury of the fascinating, frightening, entrancing and inspiring tapestry of Scotland's storytelling.

ancient scotland

Calanais

N THE WESTERN SIDE of the Isle of Lewis, overlooking Loch Roag is one of the most remarkable megalithic structures in the British Isles. This is the unique stone circle of Calanais. The landscape around it is dotted with many more megalithic sites, showing that this was an area of major importance 5,000 years ago. The location of the site by a sea loch at the westernmost edge of Europe reminds us that in that distant time traveling by water was commonplace – and much easier than traveling across the heavily wooded land mass of the continent. The monument itself is roughly the shape of a Celtic cross with a central circle, a long avenue running north-south and shorter avenues leading from the circle to east and west, though nowadays the original design is no longer complete. What is agreed amongst a wide range of scholars is that Calanais is ideally positioned to see the standstill of the moon. This is the time every 18.6 years that the moon reaches its furthest west setting and can be seen clearly in a notch of the hills to the south from the avenue of Calanais. It is not a coincidence that the hills to the south are known as caillich na mointich – usually translated as the 'old woman of the moors' but, in all probability, in ancient belief was a reference to the appearance of a sleeping goddess in the landscape. While this is remarkable in itself there is more, much more.

When Martin Martin visited the island in 1695 he was told that the site had been a place of worship in heathen times, though we should be careful of the then current fashion for linking all megalithic structures with the shadowy figures of the Druids. However, it seems he was not the first to write of this mysterious and awesome place. An ancient Greek writer told of a priest called Abaris coming to Athens round about 350AD from 'the winged temple of Apollo' in Hyperborea. Hyperborea means 'the place beyond the north wind' and is generally agreed to mean the British Isles. Many scholars have tried to make out that the reference is to Stonehenge but Calanais is in fact a much better fit. The god Apollo was said to dance at this temple every 19 years and we have already seen how Calanais was created to watch the 18.6 year cycle of the moon. Apollo is however thought of as a sun god and it is here that the local legends of Calanais begin to really matter. It has been handed down through the oral tradition that each Midsummer the 'Shining One' walks down the central avenue of Calanais. This would appear to be the Gaelic God Lugh who has, like Apollo, often been portrayed as a sun god. He is heralded by a cuckoo and it was thought that all cuckoos visiting Lewis first flew to Calanais. There is a great deal of bird lore hinted at in Celtic legend and the cuckoo was portrayed as coming to call the time for Beltain, the great ancient traditional fire festival that took place on 1 May throughout the British Isles and beyond.

A legend concerning the erection of the stones was written down by a local minister last century and it tells of a group of ships coming into Loch Roag, manned by black men. They were accompanied by priests, the chief of whom had a white cloak of bird feathers. After the stones were erected the ships and their crews left but the priests stayed behind to officiate at the stones. This is a striking story and all the more relevant because nowadays we know that the megalith builders seemed to have sailed up the coast of Europe from as far south as Morocco. All the Atlantic coastal lands have great stone creations and it is intriguing that many of them from Morocco, Galicia in north-west Spain, Brittany, Scotland and Ireland also share a love of music created on pipes and drums.

Until the 19th century some local families were known as 'of the Stones' and tradition says that they had the duty of raising the neid-fire at the Beltain ceremonies held at the stones. Neid-fire was raised by the friction of wood on wood. After all fires had been put out and after walking the bounds of village and fields people would then use the sacred fire to light their house fires. Much care was taken to ensure that the fire was properly damped down at night in such a way as to be brought to life again in the morning. If the fire went out bad luck was sure to follow and to give someone a light to restart their own fire was to give away part of your own good luck. Here as at other locations the actual raising of the neid-fire was probably a complex ritual. Such traditions lasted long, for despite the blandishments of the parish priests – and Hebrideans have long been noted for their Christian devotion – it was believed that it would be a bad thing to neglect the old stones.

Calanais has attracted other types of more general stories through its long existence. Apart from the motif of the Fir Bhreige one story told was that the local giants met to discuss what to do about the arrival of a Christian missionary – St Kieran, who, once they were gathered turned them into stone! Hardly an act of Christian kindness.

Another story tells of a great white cow that came to the stones from Loch Roag itself in a time of hardship and near famine, following a Viking raid on the island. No matter how often she was milked this white cow gave freely to everyone who brought their pail. One day a woman came with two pails and the cow, being a magical beast, asked her in Gaelic, what she was doing. The woman explained that her friend was sick and had asked her to bring her pail for milk. So the cow duly let her have two pails. This was noticed by another woman, who happened to be a witch, and greedy with it. Next day she too brought two buckets but the cow realised what was happening and only let her have the one. Angered by this, the spiteful witch returned the following day with one pail – but a pail with no bottom. In this way she milked the cow dry and the magical creature disappeared, never to be seen again.

Another tale of witchcraft concerns two young women in the locality who were in love with the same man. They had been friends but they were being driven apart by this and one of them went to consult a witch as to how she could ensure her success in winning the love of the man. The witch gave her a magic belt which she was told to give as a gift to her rival, who would then be 'taken away' by her master. This was obviously the devil and the lass, though accepting the belt began to realise what she was doing and despite being lovesick decided against harming her friend. However she had no idea how she could get rid of such a dangerous object.

At last she thought she had found a way. She went on her own late one evening to the stones of Calanais. Summoning up all her courage she took the belt and fastened it around one of the stones. The stone burst into flame and the air was filled with a great noise of howling and honking and the flapping of wings. A great cloud of smoke began together and the lass took to her heels. The next day she returned. The stone round which she had fastened the belt was broken just above where it had been clasped, the upper half of it lying on the ground and scorch marks covering the stone round the break. This was believed to be the stone just outside the circle on the east side of the southern avenue and given as number 34 in some descriptions.

The range of stories relating to Calanais is hardly surprising. Today as you approach the stones on the road from Stornoway and see them first along the ridge at Breasclete they can still take the breath away and as more and more sites in the locality are discovered, the fundamental importance of this magical place is underlined.

the Ghost of Norrie's Law

N THE NORTH SIDE of the river Forth stands Largo Law overlooking the coastal village of Upper Largo. A mile beyond the Law is the remains of an ancient burial mound, known locally as Norrie's Law, which is linked to Largo Law by a strange tale...

On the slopes of Largo Law itself the local children would play a widely known game, but with its own local slant. One child would stand in front of a group of pals and say,

'A'll tell ye a story, Aboot Tammie o Norrie, If ye dinnae speak in the middle o it, Will ye no?' The idea was simple, to make one of the other, probably younger children, say no and thus the story couldn't be told. This is a very widespread bairns' game, the difference here being the mention of Tammie o Norrie, a local cowherd who figures in the tale. There was a local tradition that a ghost haunted the slopes of Largo Law, a ghost that was condemned to roam the earth till it could unburden itself of a secret. The secret was where the robber, whose apparition now haunted the hill, had buried his gold. In life he had been an evil creature driven by the lust for gold and in death his obsession cursed him. He had no hope of attaining eternal bliss unless he could unburden himself of his secret. Many people had thought to help the poor creature by listening to his tale, and of course get some benefit for themselves for their kindness, but all, when confronted by the grim apparition in the gloaming of the shores of the Law had been unable to control their terror and had run away.

Eventually though, one local man, a shepherd on the farm of Balmain decided that he was just the boy to approach the ghost and relieve it of its burden, thereby enriching himself. Like the robber he was driven by dreams of wealth and was a sour and bitter man. Dissatisfied with his lot as a shepherd he thought he deserved better and that if he could get the buried treasure the people of the area would see his true mettle! He thought about it long and hard and then one evening, summoning up all his courage he went to Largo Law in the gloaming, hoping to meet the unfortunate spirit. Walking along the northern shoulder of the hill in the darkening light he saw what appeared to be a shimmering cloud of smoke not far in front of him. As he watched, the strange shimmering seemed to solidify and in the blink of an eye he found himself confronted by the ghost. A tall deathly looking figure it was and the spectre looked long and hard at him causing his blood to run cold. The spirit stood silent before him.

'I have come...' he stammered and fell silent, flinching under the steely gaze of the undead eyes, he steeled himself he spoke again. 'I have come to listen to your tale and help you seek eternal rest.'

The creature looked hard at him and it seemed as if a

cold vice had grabbed his heart. Then a sepulchral voice boomed out,

> 'If the Auchendowrie cock disnae craw,
> An the herd o Balmain disnae blaw,
> A'll tell ye where the gowd is on Largo Law.
> Come here on the morrow an dinnae be late
> For I'll no wait longer than the hour o eight'

At that the spirit shimmered and seemed to drift away like smoke on the soft breeze blowing off the river. The shepherd was shaking with excitement. He was going to be rich. The next day at eight o'clock he would know where the buried treasure was. All he hed to do was follow the ghost's instructions. What had he said? 'If the Auchendowrie cock disnae blaw' that was easily enough done he thought. The other bit, 'An the herd o Balmain disnae blaw' well he could sort that too. The cowherd of Balmain was Tammie o Norrie, a man he had little time, or respect for, and he was sure he could stop him blowing on his horn to summon the cattle into the byre in the early evening without too much bother.

The following morning the entire household of Auchendowrie farm slept in. No cock had cried to waken the maid to light the fore. When the farmer's wife heard this and went to check she found her prize rooster dead on the dung heap, strangled. The shepherd had been round before dawn and later was waiting to catch Tammie o Norrie as he drove his cows out to pasture. He was standing leaning on a gatepost when Tammie drove the cattle out of the byre and through the farmyard.

'Hey you, Tammie o Norrie, I want a word wi ye,' he said, looking furtively around.

Now Tammie knew who the shepherd was and was aware there were few people who had a good word to say about him but, never one to pay attention to gossip, he had nothing against the man.

'Aye, well whit is it?' Tammie asked, 'Be quick though I've tae get these beasts out tae the pasture.'

'Listen tae me. Tonight ye' had better no blaw yer horn tae summon the cows hame or it'll be the worse for ye, understand,' and he drew back his coat to reveal a long knife stuck in his belt.

'Whit dae ye mean. No blaw my horn. How will I get the cattle hame' Tammie asked, puzzled by this turn of events.

'Ye can run them in wi yer dugs,' snarled the shepherd, his hand clasping the handle of the knife and glowering at Tammie. 'Mind what I say or ye'll suffer for it,' and saying that he turned and stamped off.

Now Tammie was quite bemused by this. The man was obviously dangerous and had made it pretty clear what he wanted. However Tammie was never a man that liked to be ordered about and as he looked after the retreating figure he muttered to himself, 'Aye well, we'll see, we'll see.'

That evening the shepherd made his way to the northern slope of the hill just before eight o'clock.

Just as the wraith appeared and was about to speak,
the sound of a cow horn floated through the air from
Balmain. The ghost, deprived of its release from earthly
torment, spat out the words,

'Woe tae the man that blew that horn, Fae oot o that
spot he shall neer be borne',

and disappeared. In a blind rage the shepherd ran
to the north, the thought of killing the Balmain cowherd
pulsing in his mind. When he got to what is now the site
of Norrie's Law he was too late. There stood the figure
of Tammie Norrie, horn at his lips – turned to stone.
The local people tried to shift the unfortunate man,
but some magical force prevented them and in
desperation, and some fear, they heaped a great mound
of earth over the unfortunate cowherd. This was given
the name of Norrie's Law.

This story seems to be a degenerate version of an
even older tale that said that inside the mound was the
body of an ancient warrior called Norroway who had
been buried astride his horse in a suit of silver armour!
What we do know is that sometime in the 1830s a local
cadger, or carter, was digging sand out of the hill for
some building he was doing when he made a remarkable
discovery. He found the treasure. Over a few years he sold
most of it to a silversmith in Cupar who melted it down
and re-used it. Eventually the cadger's conscience got the
better of him and he handed over the few remnants he
had to the widow of the local landowner, the recently
deceased General Durham. She in turn donated the

material to the then Museum of Antiquities and the
few magnificent remnants of the original Norrie's Law
hoard can be seen in the new Museum of Scotland.
There are just a few bits and pieces including a pair
of pins with Pictish symbols, a couple of lozenge-shaped
pieces that once might have been part of a corselet of
mail, and pieces of a sword hilt, helmet and scabbard.

sueno's stone

N FORRES ON THE COAST of the Moray Firth there is one of the most remarkable of the Pictish Symbol Stones. Standing almost five metres high it has been suggested that this stone is possibly later than all the other Pictish stones. It is a slightly different style from most of the rest but in its obvious depiction of a battle it is not unique – the other famous battle stone being the Aberlemno Kirkyard Stone, thought by many to be a depiction of the battle of Dunnichen in 685 when the Picts slaughtered the Northumbrian Angles near Forfar. In certain areas of Scotland the Pictish stones were long thought to be Danish and there is a strong connection with Scandinavia in the story of Sueno's Stone.

Though Sueno's Stone itself was found buried in the 18th century and was then re-erected as a tale which local people told, it carries us back to what have long been called the Dark Ages. It is said that the stone commemorates a battle between the local people and an invading force of Norsemen. Fighting had been going on for many years as the Norsemen had started to settle in the area and in the struggle for overall control of Moray, the principal antagonists were Maelbrigde, the Mormaor of Moray and the Norse Jarl Sueno. Mormaor and Jarl are both terms meaning something close to High Chief. Now Maelbrigde was a famous warrior and was known throughout Scotland, the Northern Isles and much of Scandinavia as Maelbridge Bucktooth. This was because he had a strange deformity. His left eye-tooth was almost ten centimetres long and came down to just below his jawline. It was like the fang of a wild boar and had a strange mottled yellowish-reddish colour. It was rumoured that the tooth itself was poisoned and it forced the great warrior to speak with a bit of a lisp. It might have even been this facial peculiarity that had turned Maelbrigde into the fearsome warrior he undoubtedly was. No-one, Pict or otherwise would dare to pass comment on his tooth for his skill with the sword was as legendary as his great strength. Those who had mocked him in his youth did not survive to tell their tale. He was a fierce and proud warrior and his name, meaning the servant of Bride, a pagan Mother Goddess figure, before she became St Bride, the birthmaiden of Jesus in the Christian beliefs of Scotland.

By this time Maelbrigde was into his middle years and his face and body bore many scars from battles, with Vikings and Scots, and other Picts, for they were a warlike people. He was more than a great warrior though. He was a true leader of men and the Picts of Moray would follow him into the gates of hell if he commanded them. They had grown to trust in this man's strength and wisdom and most of all in his skills as a strategist. In those far off days a man's birth would do him little good if he could not wield a sword well and command the respect of his fellow tribesmen. And this respect was mutual. Bound as he was by blood-ties to many of the Picts in Moray, Maelbrigde felt it hard any time he lost a warrior in battle, and in the battles with the cursed Viking Sueno he had been losing fine young men, year after year. All through one cold, wet winter as he sat by the fire in his fort by the sea, he puzzled over what he could do to resolve the ongoing feud.

He well understood that Sueno, though a noted warrior who had the respect of his men, was utterly ruthless and would be hard to convince that peace of any kind was a good idea. He was a Viking and thought the only options for him were victory or death. Still he was a warrior and Maelbrigde thought he could settle matters once and for all. He would offer Sueno a straight fight with winner take all. Whoever triumphed would have the lordship of Moray. Sueno would never agree to fight him one on one, such was Maelbrigde's fearsome reputation. Sueno was no coward but they were few men anywhere who would have reckoned they had much of a chance against the great Pictish warrior. At last he made a decision. He would offer Sueno a battle with 20 warriors apiece. That should make it all right. It was the warrior's way.

So the following day an experienced Pictish warrior called Drostan was sent to the Viking camp to carry Maelbrigde's challenge. Approaching the Viking camp he held his hands high in the air to show he had no weapons.

The guards on the walls of Viking fort, seeing he

was unarmed, allowed the doors to be opened and two of them came out, battle-axes at the ready.

One of them spoke. 'What do you want Pict?' he asked in Norse.

Drostan answered in the same language. His command of the language, learned from his mother, who was Norse, had made him the obvious choice for this mission.

'I want to speak to Sueno. I have a message from Maelbrigde.'

After checking to see that the Pict had no concealed weapons the Vikings led him into the presence of their leader. Inside a large timber hall within the fort Sueno was sitting on a bench covered with furs. Drostan was led before him.

'Well?' demanded the Norse chief.

'My chief, the great Maelbrigde, has sent me with a message, Sueno the Viking,' the Pictish warrior said. He was brave warrior who had faced death many times in battle, but standing here unarmed in the hall of the Viking chief he felt the cold drips of sweat roll down his back.

'Maelbrigde says that every year both you and he are losing young men in these ongoing battles,' he continued.

'So what,' snarled Sueno, 'what does Bucktooth want to do? Does he want to surrender to me?' he asked with a cold smile, well aware that using the Morrmaor's nickname would anger this Pict standing before him.

Biting back a retort, Drostan simply bent his head and said, 'Maelbrigde the Mormaor challenges you to meet him in battle two weeks from the next Saturday on the beach below the Red Cliffs at low tide. He will bring 20 mounted warriors and you will do the same. Whoever wins on the day will have control over the whole of Moray. That is his challenge. What is your answer?'

As the Pict spoke, Sueno's eyes had narrowed. This was a straight forward challenge and was certainly the warrior's way of doing things, however Sueno was never one to pass up any advantage so he simply grunted, 'tell Bucktooth I will think it over.'

Then turning to one of his warriors he spat out, 'Get this piece of Pictish filth out of here.'

Gritting his teeth, Drostan was led out of the hall and through the fort's gates. Later that afternoon he returned to Maelbrigde's hill-fort overlooking the Moray forth.

'Well?' asked the Mormaor in his strange lisping voice, 'what did Sueno have to say to my challenge?'

'I am afraid he said he would think about it, that's all,' replied Drostan.

This was just about what Maelbrigde had expected. Sueno was a great warrior but it was well known that he always looked at every situation long and hard seeking to find an advantage.

'Well then,' Malebrigde smiled, 'we shall just have to wait.'

It was three days later when an unarmed Viking turned up at Malebrigde's fort.

On being shown into the Mormaor's presence he

spoke, in Pictish. 'My lord, the Great and famous Viking Sueno has deigned to accept the challenge you presented. Two weeks for this Saturday at low tide he shall meet you below the Red Cliffs. He shall bring 20 mounted warriors just as you shall. And he says he accepts that whoever wins on the day will have total control of all of Moray. Just as you suggested. And he swears this by Odin our All-father,' This last was said with something of a sneer but Malebrigde had what he wanted and he simply signalled for the Viking to be shown out.

In the week before the great battle the 20 chosen Pictish warriors were busy getting ready. Swords and spears had to be sharpened and polished, shields repaired and strengthened and as the day approached the excitement grew. The younger warriors were busy telling each other of how well they would fight on the day. The older ones just smiled and nodded. They had been in too many battles to take anything for granted. They were warriors and as ever, ready to die in battle, but they knew their end could come at any time.

So the fateful day arrived and the 21 Picts rode out in a column from the hillfort to the cheers of the rest of the community's population. All were fully armed and all had carefully cleaned and combed their hair and facial hair. It was important a warrior looked his best on such a day. They made a magnificent sight as they rode down to the beach from the cliff-top fort, the cheers of their kin echoing in their ears.

As they approached the chosen spot below the great

Red Cliffs, Maelbrigde could see a bunch of horsemen off in the distance. As they rode on he began to be able to pick out that there did seem to be about 20 of them. He scanned the cliffs above and the dunes below them. No sign of any extra Vikings there. He had been worried that Sueno might try and get up to something but everything seemed all right. On he rode and soon could clearly see that there were 21 horsemen approaching, the leader slightly ahead of the rest. But wait a minute. What was that?

On the back of every horse he could now clearly see two pairs of legs. The scheming conniving Viking had brought twice as many men as had been agreed. Maelbrigde's anger surged up through his blood. A red mist flared before his eyes at this treachery. Hauling out his sword, he waved it over his head, kicked his heels into his horse and shouted charge. Behind him the Pictish warriors reacted as one and followed on after their leader. The Picts charged straight into the Vikings. Just before Maelbrigde and his men reached them the men behind the riders leapt from the horses' backs and fanned out to surround the Picts. Each and every one of them was carrying a spear as well as his sword. As the two groups of horsemen clashed the other Vikings ran in at the exposed backs of the Picts.

It was over in minutes. Thanks to their leader's treachery the Vikings had attained a remarkable victory. All 21 Picts lay dead on the sand. A few of the Vikings were injured but none had life-threatening wounds.

Even the great Maelbrigde Bucktooth had been unable
to kill any of them such was the overwhelming numbers
and careful planning of the Vikings. They were ecstatic.
Their leader's plan had worked and all of them had
come through the battle alive. The few that had received
serious wounds were being treated by their comrades
while the others shouted and congratulated each other.
Sueno was looking down at the dead body of a hit
opponent. He had tricked the great Maelbrigde
Bucktooth and now he would be lord over the
whole land. With his sword in his right hand Sueno
reached down and grabbed the long hair of the Pictish
corpse. Yanking on the hair he pulled the upper half
of the body off the ground. With one stroke of his sword
he sliced of the Mormaor's head! His men saw what he
was doing and let out a cheer.

Sueno held up the blood-dripping head of his enemy
at the level of his own face and laughed at it, 'Well what
do you think of that trick then, Bucktooth?'

All around him his men burst into laughter, partly out
of relief, partly to cover the embarrassment they all felt at
the underhanded trick they had played on the Picts. Still
the victory was theirs.

Then one of them, emulating their leader reached
down and lopped the head off another Pictish corpse.
Whoops of laughter rang out again and another copied
him. Within seconds all 21 Pictish corpses were headless.
One or two of the younger lads among the Vikings started
throwing the heads at one another and a couple of them

starting kicking them around. And all the while Sueno
was looking at Maelbrigde's head with a smile on his face.

Then, sheathing his sword, he took the long hair of the
Pict in two bunches, tied them in a knot and walked over
to his horse, There he hung the severed head over the
pommel of his saddle! His men looked at each other –
he was going to take the Pict's head home as trophy of
war. Some of them had heard the Picts themselves had
once done such things. It seemed a good idea and the
others started dong the same. Soon all 42 of the Vikings
were sitting on horseback, and half of them had blood-
dripping, gory trophies of war hanging from the saddles
of their horses.

And so off they set towards their own home base.
Sueno, at the head of his men could hear them begin to
sing short snatches of songs and chant short lines about
the great victory they had had. If he had had a big head
before it was even bigger now as he heard the singing and
praises of his warriors riding behind him. So they set off
along the beach towards home. But unnoticed by Sueno,
caught up as he was in the success of his plan and the
praise of his Vikings, the bloody severed head of the Pict,
each time Sueno's horse's hooves hit the sand, turned just
a fraction. It was a tiny movement each time but within a
few minutes the long, discoloured buck tooth of the
Pictish leader was against the thigh of Sueno. He did not
notice a thing. Behind him several of his warriors had
brought out the horns of mead they had brought and
passed them round. The singing grew louder and Sueno's

heart swelled. Truly he was great leader. This was just the start. Now he had gained control of Moray he could start to build up his power. Soon he would move on Caithness and after that, well, the opportunities were immense now he had won this victory. Soon the troop of horsemen were in sight of their own palisaded fort. All along its ramparts the women and children and old women were lined up waiting to see how many of their husbands, fathers and brothers had survived the battle. When they realised that all 42 of them had survived the battle the whole community let out a great cheer. No one had been killed, they had all lived to tell the tale of a great victory.

On hearing the cheer Sueno hauled on his horse's reins. The great creature rose up on its rear legs its forelegs pawing at the air. Then the Viking leader dug in his heels and the horse set off in a great leap. Through the air it soared and came down with a thud on the sand. And as it came down the force of its landing sent the great head of Maelbrigde up in the air. Down it came. The tooth, the discoloured fang of Maelbrigde Bucktooth sank its full length into the thigh of Sueno the Viking. He let out a dreadful shriek. He dropped the horse's reins and yanked the head up. Out came the ominous fang. Followed by a great gut of blood. The watching crowd fell silent as Sueno threw the bloody head away from him with a roar of anger and pain. Some of the warriors came to Sueno's help. The blood was pumping out of his thigh as he roared. This was not how a Viking warrior should behave, some of them were thinking. He was dragged from his horse, a tourniquet was improvised from a sword belt and a group of the Viking warriors carried their stricken leader back to the fort at a run.

Once there they called the wisest and most experienced of the old women to see what they could do. They came with poultices and bandages but as soon as the tourniquet was released the blood pumped again. And all the time Sueno roared like a madman. Mead was brought and he grasped the horn and tossed it down,

'More mead,' he shouted as the women tried to staunch the bleeding. It took them a good while but at last they stopped the blood flowing, by which time Sueno had drunk so much mead he had fallen into a fitful sleep. So they bandaged up his leg, and covered him with furs as he lay there tossing in a fitful, mead-induced sleep, muttering and moaning. This was bad, no Viking should act as he had done. It was only pain and their warriors were raised to laugh at pain and death.

All through that night, with the old women watching over him, Sueno tossed and turned, pouring with sweat. Just before dawn he calmed down and seemed to have gone into a healthier sleep.

Then in the morning they decided to look at this leg. As they pulled back the blankets and undid the bandages a dreadful, charnel-house smell erupted. Tugging off the sodden cloths they all stood back. From the tip of his toe to the point of his groin Sueno's leg was black!

None of them, not even the eldest had ever seen

anything like this. It was as if his leg had been rotting for days! Maybe the rumours they had all heard of Maelbrigde's tooth being poisoned had been true after all. Whatever the truth of the matter nothing could be done and by that night Sueno the Viking breathed his last.

News of his death spread like wildfire amongst the peoples of Moray, Viking and Pict. The news was passed onto men heading for Norway on board ships and riders headed out with the news to the west and south. And all carried the same story. Sueno the Viking had been deserted by the Gods of the Vikings. They had allowed Maelbrigde to have his revenge even after death because of what Sueno had done. By accepting the challenge to fight with 20 men and bringing twice that number he had broken the word of the warrior and destroyed the code of honour that held the warrior's way of life together. By his treachery he had managed to kill the Pictish Mormaor and his men, but at terrible price. From that day forth not one of the men who had accompanied him on that fateful day below the Red Cliffs would ever admit to it and soon the Picts had re-established total control over Morayshire. And the local people said this is why the great stone was erected, to remind future generations of the treacherous behaviour of Sueno the Viking.

vanora's stone

ABOUT 18 MILES north east of Perth, north of the
Sidlaw Hills that run parallel to the river Tay,
lies the Strathmore village of Meigle. All too
easily ignored by the traffic going to and from
the North-east this little place contains a real treasure
for those interested in the ancient culture of Scotland.

The old school next to the Kirk on Dundee road has
been turned into a museum unlike any other. It contains
a unique and beautiful collection of Pictish Symbol Stones,
most of which are believed to have originally stood in
or near the Kirk yard. Others are possibly from the
surrounding area. One of these stones has a local legend
that links it to one of the all time great European literary
and mystical themes — the story of Arthur and Guinevere.

The stone is known to the locals as Vanora's stone
and was at one time part of a unique linked group of
symbol stones that stood in the adjoining Kirk yard,
probably on the prehistoric burial mound known as
Vanora's Mound. The name Vanora is a local variant of
the name Guinevere and this great Pictish Symbol Stone
once formed a memorial on the grave of that adulterous
queen.

On one side of the stone is a fine example of a Celtic
cross and in the middle of the other side is a gowned
figure who appears to be undergoing attack by animals.
The official guide book tells us that this is a representation

of the Biblical story, Daniel in the Lions' Den, but local legend, unconcerned with the need to explain everything in our past as being of Christian origin, tells us otherwise.

Before the French and English romanticists took the Arthurian tales and turned them into florid fancies of chivalry and honour these stories were an integral part of the P-Celtic-speaking culture that existed throughout much of the British Isles. The P-Celtic languages were Pictish, Cornish, Breton and Welsh. Like the widespread cycle of hero-tales in the related Q-Celtic languages of Scottish and Irish Gaelic that tell of the exploits of Finn MacCoul and his warriors, the Fianna, the original Arthurian legends were given local settings by the small communities that made up the tribal populations of these islands. Examples of this can be found in stories and place names from Scotland to the Scilly Isles. Our ancient tribal cultures incorporated actual historical events into great tales alongside older gods and goddesses who were given human form. And the tales were told to children for generations beyond number. To make sure the children understood the stories, they were always set within the environment they lived in, which is why we have so many variants of particular stories across this island.

The story of Vanora's Stone tells us that she was the queen of Arthur, a sixth century king. Having brought peace to the land, Arthur, like many other kings before and after him, decided to go on a pilgrimage to Rome. This was maybe to show his loyalty to the Roman church in its struggle against the independent Columbian church of that time. Before leaving he appointed his nephew (some say his bastard son) Modred to act as regent and to rule over the people in his place.

No sooner had Arthur left the country than Modred seized the throne and seduced his aunt, Vanora. Whether she was a willing victim or had planned the whole thing with Modred is unclear, but soon they were ruling Arthur's kingdom as man and wife, with warriors from among Modred's own close relations supporting their rule.

Arthur was still in southern Britain when a messenger caught up with him to tell him the news. At once he headed north to raise an army from among his own kinfolk and followers. He was set on having his revenge upon the faithless pair. The battle where Arthur and Modred met is said to have been at Camlaan, quite probably Camelon near Falkirk. Arthur was victorious but in killing the traitor Modred he himself was fatally wounded. Some stories say he was then taken to the mystic Isle of Avalon by Morgan and her eight sisters, and that he lives there still. The story told at Meigle says he soon died of his wounds and with him went any faint hope Vanora might have treasured for merciful treatment.

While Modred's actions were perhaps understandable given the nature of the times, Vanora had committed truly unforgivable sins. The tribal peoples laid great stress on the ritual and spiritual importance of their rulers and Vanora had betrayed the most sacred trust. She was guilty of both treason and adultery and her fate was a foregone conclusion – death.

The manner of her execution had to be decided however and while the deliberations continued she was imprisoned in Modred's Castle on Barry Hill, near Alyth, just a few miles north of Meigle. This was a serious business indeed and could not be rushed. At last Vanora was brought forth to hear the sentence that had been passed and it must have surpassed even her deepest fears.

So bad was her treachery to her husband, king and people that it had been decided that her death had to be as dishonourable as possible. She was to be ripped apart, limb from limb, by a pack of wild dogs! It is this grisly scene that local tradition maintains is carved on the stone.

After this brutal death, what was left of Vanora's body was buried in the Kirk yard at Meigle. All sorts of powerful curses were heaped upon her grave by both the Christian and pagan priests of Arthur's people. More than 1,200 years after her execution and burial these curses survived in local belief. It was said that any young woman foolhardy enough to walk over Vanora's Mound would immediately become incapable of having children. She would be rendered sterile on the spot! And so the faithless queen is still remembered.

castles and royalty

a dangerous man

KINGS OF SCOTLAND were often paranoid and none more so than James III. He had good cause to be! In the months after his marriage to Margaret of Oldenburg, Princess of Denmark in 1476, he became concerned that both his brothers, Alexander, Duke of Albany and John, Earl of Mar were plotting against him. He grew to believe that Alexander was even plotting with the English to overthrow James and have himself crowned as King Alexander IV. This was all too believable as Alexander, who held the position of the Warden of the Marches and was thus responsible for maintaining peace along the border with England, was a wild and dangerous man. On many occasions he mounted major raids into England, not for any sound political reason, but apparently to gather booty. In this he was assisted by a large group of men, little better than bandits, whom he had recruited from amongst the wild families of the Borders. These families, like their distant cousins in the Highlands, were addicted to the raiding way of life. Ever ready to take advantage of the chaotic situation arising from the regular outbreaks of hostilities between Scotland and England, they were a constant problem both north and south. Albany, rather than controlling them, seemed almost to have become one of them and carried out raids in

Scotland too. James was becoming increasingly angered at this and in 1482 ordered the arrest of both of his brothers. John was said to have died of a fever soon afterwards and it was rumoured that the fever itself had been caused by witchcraft, while another even grislier tale said he had been bled to death in the dungeons of Craigmillar Castle. Whatever his eventual fate, he disappeared for good shortly after being arrested. There are those who suggest that it was perhaps John's skeleton that was found walled up in the castle in 1818! Albany was committed to Edinburgh Castle where James reckoned he would be safe from any escape attempt by either his band of desperadoes or the more reckless of his supporters amongst the courtiers. While he had a faction of supporters he also had plenty of enemies at court some of whom urged the king to try him for treason and execute him. Being informed of the disappearance of his younger brother he was only too aware that the King was hardly likely to be more merciful towards him, particularly after his behaviour as Warden of the Marches. He might have been imprisoned but he was of the royal blood and had a constant stream of visitors to his rooms in the castle. These were in a long gone building known as David's Tower which stood right on the edge of the northern cliff of Castle Rock. Despite his position however he was a prisoner and only had one servant or chamber-chiel. One evening he was told by a visitor that there was a French ship that had brought a consignment of wine from Gascony anchored off Leith. If he could make his way there the captain was ready to

take him out of Scotland, the necessary bribes already
having been paid. The following day, two barrels of wine
from the Gascon ship arrived at David's Tower, and were
brought unopened to Alexander's apartments. Hidden in
one of them was a thin but strong rope and a letter.
The letter had an ominous message indeed. It said that
a group of the courtiers around the king were urging
that he should not be tried, but killed out of hand and
that the king was minded to accept their advice! There
was no time to lose. He would have to try and escape.
So that night he invited the Captain of the Guard and
his three principal officers to sample the wine that had
been delivered. They were happy to accept the invitation
and that evening they arrived, all wearing breastplates
and helmets. They took off their helmets and set to
sampling the Gascon wine and playing cards. Alexander
was careful to ensure they all drank more than he did
and after a couple of hours all four of the officers were
considerably drunk. Three of them were virtually
comatose, and the Captain of the Guard was the only
one to still have his wits about him to any extent.
Judging his moment Alexander grabbed the captain's
long dagger from his belt and stabbed him in the heart.
Again and again he stabbed him before turning his
attention to the others. Within a minute or two all had
suffered the same bloody fate. Whether fired up by blood-
lust or acting out of spite, it is impossible to say but he
and his servant threw the four bodies onto the great
roaring fire that blazed at one end of the room. Then they

headed to the top of the windowless tower carrying the rope. Tying it to the balustrade Alexander threw it over the side. His servant went first over the battlements. However he came to the end of the rope only to find himself still a distance from the ground. There was nothing to do but let go and hope for the best. He fell more than 20 feet and letting out a yell as his leg broke, rolled over, hit his head and lost consciousness. Above him Albany realised what must have happened. Not knowing whether anyone else had heard the cry he hurriedly pulled up the rope. Luckily he had thought to bar the door into the tower so he had some time if guards were coming. He ran back down to his chambers and using the captain's blood-encrusted dagger quickly cut his sheets and blanket into strips. By now sweating profusely he hardly noticed the stench of the burning bodies that was beginning to fill the tower. Again he returned to the top of the tower and tied the sheets and blankets to the end of the rope, before once more flinging it over the battle-ments. The rope was now just long enough and soon he was standing at the foot of Castle Rock. In the darkness he could see that his servant was not only unconscious but that his leg was lying at a funny angle. Then, showing a concern and humanity that was the exact opposite of his behaviour just a short time earlier, he hoisted the man on his shoulders and set off to Leith. Whatever could be said of Albany he was a strong and fearless man and when he put his mind to something he did it. Once in Leith he soon found a boat to take him and his injured servant out to the Gascon boat. By dawn he was safely out in the North Sea.

When the king heard of his brother's escape and the horrendous carnage he had left behind him he did not believe it till he had visited David's Tower for himself. There he saw the unfortunate guards' bodies roasting like tortoises in their shells, as an earlier historian described it.

Albany went to France but finding himself unable to convince the French king, Louis XI to help him against his brother, departed for England where he was sure he would get help to depose James. Right enough Edward IV, as ready as any other English king to attack Scotland, entered into a treaty with Alexander at Fotheringay in June 1482. He showed his true colours in agreeing to become the King of Scotland under the suzerainty or control of Edward, something, like the earlier John Balliol who had similarly done homage to Edward I nearly a century earlier, he could never fulfil. Alexander's faction amongst the nobles in Scotland, hearing that he was coming north with a large army led by the Duke of Gloucester, later King Richard II of England, seized James and let it be known they would recognise Alexander as king, but not if he came into Scotland with Gloucester. There was great deal of communication between the various parties and in the end a truce was declared between the two countries, James was re-installed as king, Alexander was pardoned, all his lands and property restored and he was created the earl of Mar and Garioch. Alexander however could not help himself and was soon dealing with the English behind James's back again. While in England he was denounced as a traitor and condemned to death in Scotland. Again he came north on a raid into Scotland but was defeated by a force loyal to James at Lochmaben and fled to France where he met his death in a fitting manner – being accidentally killed at a jousting tournament. His elder brother only survived him for three years before falling to an assassin's knife during a battle with his still rebellious nobles. Such were the ways of kings and their kin in Scotland's Middle Ages.

couttie and the king

OW SCOTLAND'S KINGS and queens have a dramatic and often bloody history. But there are also tales of them that show them to be not really that different from the rest of us, which is of course plain fact. James V, the father of Mary Queen of Scots was a man who, though raised as a king, had a place in his heart for the people of the country. Back then in the 16th century there were men who roamed the country known as Blue Gowns or Gaberlunzies. They were men who were licensed beggars and were also known as bedesmen. Their role was to give prayers for the king and for those who gave them alms. They were given their blue gowns on the authority of the king and there was one for every year of the king's age. However James V had a wee wrinkle. Now and again he would put on a blue gown himself and travel the land just to see how things were. And sometimes he would just travel around as an ordinary person. So it was one time that he was on the road near the Cairn o Mount and met up with a man from Dundee called Couttie. Now Couttie dealt in cattle and was on his way to Deeside to pick up some cattle from a man he had dealt with before. With him he had his faithful dog, a deerhound of considerable size. At this period there was always the danger of running into what were known as 'sturdy beggars', robbers, and Couttie, like the king himself was armed with a sword and a staff. They were both heading north and it seemed to make sense for them to go together, just in case.

Now they hadn't long met and were chatting away when suddenly a gang of sturdy beggars came at them from the woods alongside the road. Now Couttie was a strong young man, as was the king and at once they defended themselves and the dog too went at their attackers. In seconds a couple of their assailants hit the ground and the others backed off, briefly. Then they came again. It was clear they thought these two travellers had money about their persons. Couttie was not the man to surrender though and he and the king fought furiously. They were being slowly driven back when Couttie was surprised to hear his travelling companion shout, 'Fight on Couttie, fight on, the face of the King is terrible!'

He had no idea what the man was going on about. However their assailants maybe did for they backed off a little. Like so many thieves through the ages they were always keen to puck up what they could get, but courage was not really a strong point. They had heard that the king was maybe in the area on his travels. They had also heard that wherever the king went there was always a band of mounted soldiers not far away. They had no intention of being cut down by the king's soldiers, or even worse, being captured and strung up by the neck! So, discretion being very much the better part of any thief's valour, they turned and ran. Couttie was bit puzzled.

'Well done, Couttie,' said James holding out his hand, 'you fought very well.'

'Aye, aye, are you alright?' replied Couttie, shaking his hand, 'but why did they run away? And what was all that about the face of the king?'

'Ah yes, that,' smiled James, 'that is because, I am the king.'

Couttie twigged immediately that this smiling man was not kidding and having heard how kings like to be fawned over, sucked up to and generally bowed down to, he fell to one knee and bowed his head.

'No, No, Couttie lad. You do not bow to me even if I am your king, for we are brothers in arms are we not?' and he pulled the astonished Couttie to his feet. It was only a few minutes later that the King's Guard who had not been that far off, rode up. But without Couttie's help they would have been too late to defend their king. And James was delighted to have had such a man as Couttie by his side in time of danger. The upshot of it was that he granted Couttie land in the very heart of his home town Dundee. And if you want to check it out, the name survives in Couttie's Wynd, the lane that runs up the backs of the buildings on Whitehall Street and Union Street to this day.

the Black Dinner

EVER SINCE WILLIAM WALLACE had rallied the Scots against Edward Longshanks, King of England in the closing years of the 14th century, the Douglas family had held a noted place in Scotland. Sir William Douglas had fought alongside Wallace in his guerrilla campaign and on the battlefield and his reputation as a brave and resourceful warrior passed on to succeeding generations. His family grew greatly powerful in the land and were often seen as a danger, and not just by the monarchs. They were equally feared by those amongst the leading families who sought to further their own power. Intrigue and plotting were a way of life amongst the so-called aristocracy of Scotland in the Middle Ages. Much was spoken of honour, but there were many black-hearted and back-stabbing deeds that those words shielded. Perhaps no episode in the period shows the blood-thirstiness of the time so much as the fate of the 16-year-old William Earl of Douglas in 1440. He had succeeded to the title on the death of his father Archibald who had died in June that year. Archibald had been appointed lieutenant-governor of the kingdom on the Coronation of James II, at the age of seven in 1439. Douglas was feared and hated by the official Regent Sir Alexander Livingstone of Callender and the Chancellor, William Baron of Crichton, and this

hatred extended to his successor, William. Both of them
were extremely ambitious but were united in their hatred
and fear of Archibald and his power. With their great
landownership and the hundreds of armed men always
available to them from the Border lands of Annandale and
Galloway, the Earls of Douglas were powerful indeed.
And they knew it. Archibald had shown his contempt for
both Regent and the Chancellor when he said, 'They are
both alike to me, it is no matter which may overcome,
and if both perish the country will be the better; and it
is a pleasant sight for honest men to see such fencers
yoked together.'

When Archibald died in June 1440, of natural causes,
the biggest obstacle to the soaring ambitions of Crichton
and Livingstone was removed. But they still had to deal
with William, who although only 16 at the time, had been
raised to take over the great power of the Douglas family.
He could call upon the loyalty of many and was a natural
focus for those who were opposed to the machinations of
Crichton and Livingstone. They were further alarmed
when William began to act only as a young man caught
up in the splendour of power and the trappings of power
and wealth that were suddenly his to command. He took
to appearing in public with a large company of heavily
armed, well mounted and magnificently equipped men.
He also took the opportunity to send Sir John Fleming
and Sir John Lauder of the Bass to the court of the French
king to ask for a new charter for lands that had been
given to his grandfather by Charles V. This was clearly

a young man who had every intention of exercising all the power and authority he could command. The Chancellor and the regent had hoped that, with the death of Archibald, they would have no trouble with the Douglas family for a while and were in a quandary. Any open attack on William would most likely plunge the whole country into Civil War. They did not want to take on the power of the Douglases head on. The country had only just settled down after the troubles that had arisen from the assassination of James I. But something had to be done, however, to reign in this ambitious and headstrong young man. Some have said that they included James Douglas, the Earl of Avondale and Wiliam's great-uncle, in the plot.

Now after the assassination of his father and the consequent turmoil in the country it had been felt that the best, and safest, place for the boy-king to be brought up was Edinburgh Castle. It was the biggest and best defended castle in the country, and the wily Crichton had effectively separated James from his mother and her courtiers who lived a mile away at Holyrood Palace, forever citing the need for absolute safety, and after Archibald's death he and Livingstone had the king under their own control. From their base in the country's greatest stronghold the Chancellor and Regent hatched a plan to solve the problem with the Douglases. They knew how dangerous their actions would be but in those bloody times, decisiveness was always seen as a virtue.

An invitation was sent to William at his home at

Restalrig, just a couple of miles from the Castle. Couched in the most glowing terms it invited the Earl of Douglas, and his younger brother David, to a dinner with his sovereign James II at the Castle on the 24 November 1440. Perhaps it was the confidence of youth, or maybe William truly thought that Crichton and Livingstone were interested in his opinion as to the future of the country, we will never know, but William accepted the invitation. He turned up at the castle with his usual company of attendant soldiers but entered the castle with only his brother and one other companion, Malcolm Fleming of Cumbernauld, a trusted adviser of his father's. He at least should have known better than to enter the lion's den so boldly! It is possible he did but that William's headstrong temperament over-ruled the sagacity of the older man. As it was there were only three of them who entered the castle that night.

Once they were in the castle the portcullis was gently lowered and the great gates quietly shut as they made their way up to the king's apartments. Here they greeted their sovereign, still only ten years old, and were seated at a great table groaning with silver and gold plates and dishes. A truly sumptuous banquet of several courses was served up. Then towards the end of the meal the atmosphere changed in an instant. As they sat there chatting with their young king William looked up to see two servants bringing in a large silver platter. On it was a black bull's head – an ancient symbol meaning only one thing. Death! The three men leapt to their feat, drawing their swords. Immediately the room was filled with fully armed and armoured men. As the young king shouted for it all to stop the Fleming and the Douglas boys were overpowered and dragged out of the chamber. There in the Castle, where the barracks now stand, under the stars they were beheaded without delay, Crichton and Livingstone looking on and ignoring the entreaties of James II. There was not even the pretence of a show trial. The Chancellor and the regent had decided that Douglas must die. A poem form the time tells of the widespread revulsion that arose in Scotland when news of the Black Dinner spread through the country.

> 'Edinburgh Castell, toun and tour,
> God grant ye sinke for sinne;
> And that even for the black dinour,
> Earl Douglas gat therein.'

If Crichton and Livingstone thought this would consolidate their power and lead to peace they could not have been more wrong. Incensed by this treachery the Douglas family and their friends rose in arms against them. Under the leadership of Earl of Avondale who had succeeded to the leadership of all the Douglases as the seventh Earl of Douglas and Angus, the struggle for control of the young king continued and the country was in an almost constant state of turmoil for years. James II himself grew to fear and hate the Douglases and was instrumental in the death of James's son William, the eighth earl of Douglas and

Angus at Stirling Castle in 1552. However the Black Dinner is probably the most notorious episode in the entire history of Edinburgh Castle.

for love of the prince

N HIS WAY SOUTH towards Edinburgh in September 1745, Prince Charlie had stopped with his army in Dunblane. In the town, he stayed in Strathallan's Lodgings in Millrow. One of the servant lasses there, Effie, was given the task of polishing his boots. Late at night after the Prince was asleep she came into his room to get the boots. Looking at the sleeping Prince her heart was filled with emotion and she could not bear to tear herself away. So she sat and polished his boots by the light of a candle. In the morning he awoke to see her still sitting there gazing at him wide-eyed. He reached out his hand towards her but she flushed and fell to her knees, still holding one of his boots.

'Come lass, and take my hand,' he smiled at her.

Effie could not bring herself to speak or even take the offered hand and simply contented her self with kissing his boot her face bright red and her eyes glistening.

'What is wrong lass?' He went on, 'are you scared of me?'

'Och no my Prince. Och no that's not it at all. I am scared to my heart for you. You are going against the English and there are ten of them for every one of your own men. I fear for you my Prince.' She lowered her head and muffled a sob.

'You need not worry, my dear,' the Prince said, 'once I have gone into England there are many there who will come forward to support my father's cause. Do not worry yourself.'

She got to her feet, put down the boot she had been holding and curtsied to the Prince before scampering from the room. Charles Edward Stewart smiled to himself. This was good sign he thought, that even the servants are supporting us. However he had much on his mind and soon forgot all about Effie.

In January the following year the Jacobite army came to Dunblane again. This time, even though they had just defeated another British Army under General Hawley at Falkirk, they were in retreat. The troops were grim-faced and tired looking. Behind them came the great army of the Duke of Cumberland, set on destroying what he saw as a treasonous rebellion by ingrates and savages. And as they came they looted and pillaged at will. As far as the Duke was concerned, all of these Scots were traitors to his father and deserved whatever they got. He was already, even at the young age of 24, a man of brutal simplicity and utter arrogance.

He too came to Dunblane and stayed overnight in the town. In the morning two men who had been caught stealing from the army baggage train were brought before him in his lodgings. They were a rough-looking pair, both dressed in the simple hodden grey that was almost a uniform for the common people of then. Both of them were firmly held by a soldier on each side.

'Right,' he said, pointing at one of the men, 'What is your name?'

'B-B-B-Brown, Your Highness,' stuttered the man,

'Ah, good. Brown,' said the Duke, 'that is a good English name. We have many Browns in our troops.' He smiled and turned to his aide-de-camp, 'Let this man go free.'

The aide-de-camp nodded to the soldiers holding Brown and he was marched out of the room.

'Now you,' he barked, pointing at the remaining man, 'what is your name?'

'My name is McNiven Sire,' replied the man, bowing his head.

'McNiven, McNiven,' roared the duke, 'That is a filthy thieving Highland name. Take him out and hang him.'

McNiven's head shot up and looked at the Duke who waved his hand and as the man's legs collapsed under him with fear, he was dragged out by the soldiers. They dragged him to a nearby tree and with no further ceremony strung him up as his companion looked on, a free man.

Returning to his breakfast as if nothing had happened Cumberland calmly finished his meal. Then he stepped outside and mounted his magnificent grey charger.

Waving to his officers to follow him he headed off eastwards along Millrow. As he went he passed by Strathallan's Lodging. Just as he got there a figure appeared in a window above him. It was Effie. In her hands she had a pan of boiling oil. Quickly she leaned out of the window and tipped the pan. The searing liquid poured down missing Cumberland by a couple of inches. It didn't miss his horse. The poor creature let out a terrified squeal and reared up, throwing his rider into the dirt. As he sprawled in the street the officers behind him started shouting, 'After her, after her. Surround the building.'

Soldiers battered down the door of the Lodgings as others ran in either direction to get round the back of the house. Boots thundered up the stairs to the room where the potential assassin had stood. There was no-one there. By the time the rest of the soldiers reached the back of the house Effie had made her escape by ducking into the underground culvert through which Mannie Burn ran to the Allan Water and escaped into open countryside. Behind her, the troops fanned out through the houses on either side of Strathallan's Lodging smashing doors and windows as they went. They found nothing and proceeded to wreck the three houses. Things would have been even worse for Dunblane had not Cumberland himself ordered his men to stop. He had given his word to the local Laird, Drummond, a staunch Hanoverian, that Dunblane would not be torched, and despite the attempted assault, he stuck to his word.

As for Effie, she got clean away. Once all the troubles had settled down she married a wealthy local farmer and lived a long and happy life, giving birth to several children, but never forgetting the effect Prince Charlie had had on her in her youth.

There has long been a local tradition that Prince Charlie left a special present behind him in Dunblane. A present that nine months later came into the world as a healthy baby boy, who went on to become a minister of religion in Glasgow and who never denied his parentage.

the scottish regalia and the wizard of the north

IR WALTER SCOTT WAS a remarkable man. While practising as a lawyer in his mid-20s, he took to writing. He drew upon his deep interest in Scottish history and culture to bring out The Minstrelsy of the Scottish Border, a three volume collection of ballads and poems from his native Border area. In 1805 he went on to achieve world-wide fame with the publication of his first collection of poetry the Lay of the Last Minstrel, which also drew on his interest in Scotland's past. However it was as a novelist that he is best remembered. His first novel Waverley, published in 1814 was written to raise much-needed cash. Due to an over-commitment to publishing he was in substantial debt and over the next few years, as his popularity grew throughout the English-speaking world, his output was prodigious. Many of his early novels were based on Scottish history, even if it now appears a peculiarly Romantic vision of Scotland's past and there is no doubt that he was the first truly great historical novelist. His works are still read today and throughout much of the 19th and 20th centuries his works were accepted to be of major importance. The great American writer Mark Twain even went so far as to blame Sir Walter Scott for the American Civil War. Twain reckoned that the gentlemen of the south were raised on Scott's Romantic ideas of fighting for a noble cause and thus went into a war against superior forces that they could never win. Scott's interest in the history of his native land, no matter how odd it may appear in the modern world, was deep and sincere. In 1818, having been researching the period around the Treaty of Union he became aware that the Crown and Regalia of Scotland had not been seen since those troubled times. He therefore decided to try and find them.

The Honours of Scotland as they are also known, consist of the Crown, the Sceptre and the Sword of State. The Crown dates from before 1540 when it was remodelled for the coronation of James V, the Sword, a gift from the Pope, dates from 1507 and the sceptre is even older. The Honours were first used together in 1543 at the bizarre coronation ceremony of the nine-month old Mary Queen of Scots. While their value as both precious items and historical artefacts is considerable, to Sir Walter they had another, deeper significance. The Honours were last used in 1650 when Charles II was crowned as King of Scots at Scone, after the English Parliamentarians under Cromwell had hacked off the head of his father, Charles I on 30 January 1649, and abolished the monarchy in England at a stroke. Cromwell arrived in Scotland from Ireland not long after, and though, due to his sympathy with Scottish Presbyterianism, his Scottish campaign was not as brutal as the one against the Catholics in Ireland had been. His vicious ravaging of Ireland left deep scars

and if things were not as bad in Scotland, they were bad
enough. By a stroke of good fortune he was victorious at
the Battle of Dunbar on 3 September, just when he was on
the point of retreating from Scotland. From then on his
luck changed and soon he had subdued most of the country. After the Battle of Dunbar, the Scots opposed to him
received intelligence that the Lord Protector, as he styled
himself, was set on getting his hands on the Honours
of Scotland. It seems he had been led to believe that
they were both more items, and of much greater value,
than they truly were. They were of course, of great
significance to the Scots, regardless of their monetary
value. They were a symbol of the country's independence
and what we would nowadays call national identity.
So they were sent off to be stored in Dunottar Caste,
a massive and awe-inspiring fortress on the east coast,
south of Aberdeen. However Cromwell soon found out
where they were and a force was sent to lay siege to
Dunottar and get the jewels! Ogilvy of Barras was in
command of the great fortress and knew well that,
even with his cannons and the New Model Army he had
created, Cromwell would be very lucky to break his way
into the massive castle. However, isolated on a spit
of land as it is, Dunottar always had one weakness.
As long as a besieging army had the patience to wait,
and could stop ships supplying the defenders from the
sea, the garrison could be starved out. Once the English
army had arrived and isolated the castle, Ogilvy needed
a plan. He discussed the matter with the Reverend Dr

Grainger, minister at nearby Kineff and like many
clergymen of the time, heavily involved in the ongoing
battle against the English Parliamentarian Army.
Grainger thought that they should include his wife in
the discussions having a high regard for her intellect.
And so a plan was formed. First a rumour was started
that the Honours had been sent to the Continent to keep
them safe. Now Mr and Mrs Grainger had a safe conduct
through to the castle and she asked if she could remove
several bundles of lint that she owned and claimed she
needed. She explained to the English commander that
times were hard and they needed money to feed their
children. The lint was hers and she wanted to sell it.
Her ploy worked and she was given leave to bring out
a handcart with the bundles of lint. It must have been
an exciting episode for her as she left the great walls of
the castle pushing her handcart in which the Honours of
Scotland were well hidden. Once she was back home she
and her husband waited till the dead of night then
sneaked out to the church. Here they buried the jewels
under the floor boards at the bottom of the pulpit.
Months later when the castle at last surrendered, there
was uproar. Where were the jewels? Threats and even
torture gave up no more information than that most
people thought they were long gone to the Continent.
The English Army had to leave empty-handed.

A few years later in 1660 Charles II was restored to
the crowns of both Scotland and England and the
Honours were returned with all ceremony to Edinburgh

by Ogilvy. He and his son were both rewarded and honoured but the Graingers, for all their loyalty and commitment, as Sir Walter Scott himself wrote, got 'the hare's foot to lick.' That is, absolutely nothing. Their central role in the saving of the Regalia was ignored! Charles of course did not last that long as monarch and was himself deposed in 1688. Tensions between the countries of Scotland and England remained high into 1707 as the Treaty of Union became imminent. Rumours flashed around Edinburgh that the Honours of Scotland were to be removed to London. Given that the Union was only forced through by bribery and coercion, and that the vast majority of the Scottish people were strongly against unification with the ancient enemy, such a move would have been dangerous. The common people of Edinburgh were always ready to riot and in the tense period leading up to the signing of the Treaty of Union, such a riot could have sparked off trouble throughout the whole country. It was therefore explicitly stated in the Act of Union that the Honours of Scotland were to remain in the country for all time, which in government speak probably had the sub-text, till they could be safely moved. In a solemn ceremony, representatives of the Three Estates who made up the Scottish Parliament watched as the Crown, the Sceptre and the Sword of State were ceremoniously locked up in the great black kist, or chest, that they are still housed in.

Over the ensuing years there was much to think about as the Union began to take hold and in time the Honours

were forgotten about. Until Walter Scott took an interest.
He was fascinated by the idea that these ancient symbols
of Scottish nationhood were still somewhere within the
Castle. Now Scott was both a Unionist and a proud Scot,
something that today seems anomalous to many, though
there are still people who claim to be precisely that!
In 1817 he petitioned Prince Regent, later King George IV
to search for them. The Regent was already an admirer
of Scott's, going so far as to make him a baronet a couple
of years later, so was happy to oblige. He therefore set up
a Commission to locate the Scottish Honours under the
guidance of Scott. So it was that one day with a goldsmith,
the Governor of the Castle broke into the room in the
bowels of the castle that had been locked since 1707.
There in the bottom of the black kist, wrapped in linen,
were the Honours of Scotland. This is how he described
it in a letter to a friend,

> The extreme solemnity of opening sealed doors of oak
> and iron, and finally breaking open a chest which had
> been shut since 7 March 1707, about a hundred and
> eleven years, gave a sort of interest to our researches,
> which I can hardly express to you, and it would be very
> difficult to describe the intense eagerness with which
> we watched the rising of the lid of the chest, and the
> progress of the workmen in breaking it open, which
> was neither an easy nor a speedy task. It sounded very
> hollow when they worked on it with their tools,
> and I began to lean to your faction of the Little Faiths.
> However, I never could assign any probable or feasible

reason for withdrawing these memorials of ancient independence; and my doubts rather arose from the conviction that many absurd things are done in public as well as in private life, merely out of a hasty impression of passion or resentment. For it was evident the removal of the Regalia might have greatly irritated people's minds here, and offered a fair pretext of breaking the Union, which for thirty years was the predominant wish of the Scottish nation.

Scott was delighted to have located the Regalia and within days they were put on display and they have been open to public view ever since.

myths and legends

atholl BROSE

IVEN THE SUBLIME nature of whisky it is little wonder that over the years it has been used as a flavouring for a range of delicacies and as a main ingredient of others. Although the life of the average Scots a few hundred years ago may have been a bit coarse by today's standards, if you made your own whisky, or had a ready access to it a plentiful supply would generally be to hand and there would be no need to be overly precious about using it in a variety of ways. One of the better known whisky recipes is Athole Brose and here is one particular recipe.

Ingredients

3 rounded tablespoons of medium oatmeal
2 tablespoons heather honey
Scotch whisky

Method

The oatmeal is prepared by putting it into a basin and mixing with cold water until the consistency is that of a thick paste. Leave for half an hour and then put through a fine strainer, pressing with a wooden spoon to extract as much liquid as possible. Throw away the oatmeal and use the creamy liquor from the oatmeal for the brose.

Mix four dessert spoonfuls of pure honey and four sherry glassfuls of the prepared oatmeal and stir well. (Purists insist on a silver spoon for stirring!) Put into a quart bottle and fill with malt whisky; shake before serving.

Now it should be said that there is absolutely no need to have access to a silver spoon. This is a drink to be drunk in all kinds of houses. However it being a Scottish drink there is of course a story as to its origin...

Long, long ago in Athole, nowadays the upper parts of the Perthshire, there was a giant. Now giants were relatively common back in the day but this one was a real pest. He had nothing but contempt for humans and saw nothing wrong with preying upon such puny creatures. So he would help himself to anybody's cattle, anytime. He was also likely to turn up and gather the whole of an entire grain store into his enormous sack. As everybody had to grow enough food to feed themselves in those days it no wonder that many brave men, and women, tried their best to stop the giant stealing their precious stores or cattle. As a result many died, and often enough the giant ended up wiping out entire communities. Often they would not be found for some time. There were far too many instances of somebody coming to visit an isolated Highland clachan only to find the mangled bodies of its inhabitants strewn around and the grain store burst open and empty. Others simply ended up starving to death or barely surviving through the help of neighbouring clachans, who themselves lived close to the edge of self-sufficiency.

The giant was a terrible blight on the country but strangely enough he had a daughter. She was more like a tall human than an actual giant and was exceedingly beautiful, with long black hair, flashing brown eyes, a curvaceous figure and a brilliant smile. Of her mother there was no sign. Her life however was pretty lonely and though the giant loved her, she longed for company of people her own age, though truth to tell she would have liked any company at all. The only others she ever met were the occasional visiting giants, most of whom were, like her father, boorish and ill-tempered. Though coming from giant parents she was in all ways much more like a human and her heart hoped one day that she might be lucky enough to find herself a husband. But how? No human would come near her, or so she thought.

Due to the giant's depredations the bens and glens around the beautiful wee valley where he and the lass lived were empty of humans. Only the occasional brave soul would venture into the area, chasing stray cattle or goats, and very, very occasionally some brave young lad would come up to the high mountain passes to hunt deer. So it was that a young lad called Dougal was out hunting in the hills one day. He knew he was near to where the giant had his dwelling and had half a mind that if he could locate his home, he could return with a large force of men and ambush the ogre- if they caught

him by surprise they could maybe put an end to him
and all the trouble he caused. So it was that he came out
of the woods on the hill above the giant's great crumpled
heap of a home. From a distance it just looked like a vast
heap of rocks. If there wasn't smoke coming from the
hearth inside most folk wouldn't give it a second glance.
However as Dougal looked down into the wee glen he
saw a movement. Thinking it might be a fine stag he
threw himself to the ground and slowly raising his head,
peered down. There between the great jumbled rock
mass and the fine sparkling burn that ran about 30 yards
from it, he saw a young woman. And what a woman!
With the keen eye of one raised to the hunt he clearly
saw not just a female but a young female and more than
that, an absolute beauty. Then as the wind shifted he
heard her singing. It was a sad, almost keening song
that rose up on the air and the voice itself was glorious.
He was transfixed as the lass went to the stream, filled
the bucket she was carrying and returned to what he now
realised must be the giant's dwelling. He had just decided
to brave things out by going to the house and speaking
to the lass when he heard a great roar. Lying perfectly
still he slowly turned his head and looked down the glen.
There, striding up the path was the giant, his great sack
bulging over his shoulder. As he watched the lass came
out and her father showed her the contents of his pack.
There were cattle, goats, chickens, geese and bags and
bags of oats and barley, enough to keep several clachans
going for the winter. Dougal's heart was no longer filled

with longing for the lass but for hatred for this vile creature who was continually wreaking havoc amongst the people of Athole. Once the giant had bundled up his booty into the sack and gone into his house with the lass, Dougal rose up and headed home his head filled with thoughts of how he could rid the world of this giant. True he had fallen for his daughter but the need to rid Athole of this curse was becoming his main desire.

Over the coming weeks his family and friends noticed that he had gone quiet. Most of them thought he had fallen for some lass but they had no idea of what was going on. He thought again of ambush but realised that such a plan might bring the giant's daughter into danger too. He knew fine well that he didn't want her harmed, he wanted to make her his own. Courtship though was not an option, he would just have to get rid of her father first then trust to fortune that he could make the lass accept him. But how was he to get rid of the giant? Then he remembered. On one of the well-worn paths near to the giant's home he had come across a great stone that was hollowed out. It was twice the size of the biggest iron cauldron he had ever seen and he remembered wondering if this was some sort of cup that the giant might use. There was one way to find out. He had a plan.

Now although he was young he was a lad of some intelligence and like many Highlanders was fond of both whisky and had a bit of a sweet tooth. He was prepared to take a bet that the giant was much the same. So for three nights he made the journey to the great stone.

The first night he was carrying two ankers or small barrels of whisky, the second night a great sack of the finest ground oatmeal and on the third night another anker of whisky and a great earthen ware pot full of the finest heather honey. In the morning after his third trip he was up at dawn and poured the ingredients into the hollow in the stone then using one of the now empty whisky barrels he brought water from a nearby stream.

Then using a thick branch cut from a tree he stirred the ingredients till they began to froth. Then, just as the heady aroma of the brew began to fill his nostrils he heard a noise. It was the giant coming through the woods from his house. Dougal barely had time to throw the barrels, sack and pot into the bushes and dive in after before the giant came into sight. Coming down the path the giant came up to the stone. Just as it looked as if he was going to stride right passed, he stopped, crinkled his nose and took a deep breath. He let out a great 'Hmmmm,' and turned to look around. Spotting the great cauldron-like boulder he bent over it and sniffed again. This time the sound that erupted was a mighty 'Ahaaaa', which caused all the birds within at least a hundred yards to take off in flight. The giant leant down and took a sip of the frothing brew.

He let out a great whoop and picking up the great, grey stone he began to drink the delectable mixture. He kept on drinking till he emptied the vessel. Then he wiped his hand over his mouth, gave a great belch, then a wild laugh and throwing the boulder to one side

he headed off down the glen. At once he began to sing.
Well that's what Dougal thought it was. In truth it
was horrible, growling noise, like boulders clashing in
a tumbling burn, but the way the giant was soon waving
his hands about, Dougal reckoned he was feeling happy.
And so he should, he had three barrels of whisky inside
him! The giant began to stride even faster and Dougal
was soon having to run to keep him in sight. As the giant
came further and further down the mountain Dougal
began to have doubts. He had no idea how much whisky
a giant could take, what if it just made him even wilder
than usual? He hadn't thought about that. Just as he
began to get frightened by what he had done he noticed
that the giant had slowed down. Then as he hid behind
a tree he noticed a wee stagger. Then another. Soon the
giant had slowed right down and was knocking over
trees as he bumped into them. His plan appeared to be
working! Within a couple of minutes the giant tripped
and fell. He pulled himself up into a sitting position
with his back against a great oak tree and within a minute
or two was fast asleep. His snore rang out like thunder
through the forest. Now Dougal had his chance.
With the thundering noise ringing in his ears, he was
sure the great creature was deep into a drink-induced
sleep. So drawing his sword he came down the path.
Without hesitation he came up beside the giant and
drove his sword right through the beast's great hairy
ear and into his brain. The giant never felt a thing as
the life left his body and the great thundering snores fell

silent. Dougal had done it. He had got rid of the Giant
of Athole. He knew he would be a hero to all the people
of Athole but what would the daughter think.

He headed straight backup the mountain to find out.
When he told her what he had done she realised that her
old life was gone for ever. And Morag, for that was her
name, realised that this young man had opened up
a whole new life for her. And though brought up by
a great, uncouth giant, she was a woman and could
see in Dougal's eyes that he was deeply in love with her.
So she consented to leave her high mountain home and
head down into Athole with the young man. Dougal was
of course considered a great hero when people heard of
his exploit and they though it all the better that when
they told the story of how he had conquered the giant,
to give this story its real true flavour, they had to serve
Athole Brose.

stoneputter's challenge

N THE REAL OLD TIMES Fionn MacCoul and his
warrior companions, the Fianna, used to live in
the great fort on the summit of Knockfarrel.
From here they would head out on their great
hunting trips all across the north of Scotland.
The Fianna were much, much bigger than the biggest
humans today but they were not the only people of
considerable stature in Scotland in those times. Not far
off from Knockfarrel there lived a giant. Like many of his
kind he spent a great deal of his time standing on his own
hill and throwing giant boulders all over the country.
This is why Scotland is covered in so many massive stones
and from their number it would seem these giants were
truly committed to their sport! Anyway, the giant was
aware of the reputation of these supposed great heroes
living in Knockfarrel and decided he would challenge
their leader to a contest. And what other kind of contest
would a Scottish giant want to take part in but chucking
boulders. He himself was so well known for this activity
that they called him Stoneputter.

One day he turned up at the great gates of Knockfarrel
and shouted out his challenge. Now Fionn was a man
who had a considerable opinion of his own worth and
he didn't see why he should have to stoop to taking part
in a contest with a simple local giant. After all he was

Fionn MacCoul, famous in many lands for his courage
and strength. So he asked which of his men would take
up the giant's challenge. Now having seen that Fionn
himself would not feign to compete with such a creature,
none of the warriors could see why they should be put
in such an undignified position. All the time they were
discussing this, Stoneputter was at the great gates of
the fort bellowing out his challenge, and after a while
beginning to hint that the inhabitants of the fort might
not be all that they were reputed to be. Now this was
serious. Fionn couldn't put up with having his own
honour and that of the Fianna called into question.
Yet he had said he would not dignify the giant with
a response and could not back down in front of his men.
Nor could he command any of them to do a thing he
would not do himself, that would really be dishonourable
and could lead to a lot of trouble. Now Fionn had an odd
knack. If he needed to understand anything he simply had
to bite his thumb. He had, as a boy tried to put down
a blister with his thumb on the Salmon of Knowledge
he was cooking for a druid. The upshot of that was that
he could access all the wisdom of the ages, and even see
the future a bit, just by biting his thumb.

He was just about to do it when his dwarf spoke up.

'Och, Fionn, why not let me take on this giant. I can
soon shut him up, no doubt,' growled the dwarf in his
deep, rumbly voice. At once Fionn saw the sense of this
and sent the dwarf out to confront the giant. He might
have been a dwarf amongst the Fianna but he was bigger

than any man around these days. Although he still hardly reached the giant's waist.

But a challenge was a challenge, thought the giant, certain he would beat this little one and demand a better man the next time. He was sure he could keep beating the Fianna till at last Fionn himself would have to come out and have a go. Stoneputter too was a creature with a high opinion of his own worth.

'All right then,' he shouted at the dwarf and picked up a great boulder – one that three normal men would not be able to move – and threw it high into the air. Out and out it soared from the summit of Knockfarrel and came to the earth with a great thud just at the eastern edge of where Strathpeffer now sits. This is the stone the Picts then carved with the Eagle.

'Huh,' grunted the dwarf, 'you think that's something? Watch this.'

And with surprising speed he ran to the great gates of Knockfarrel and one after another he pulled out the massive stone posts, – neither of which could be lifted by seven human men – and threw them one after the other to land on either side of the first stone. Stoneputter was crestfallen and slunk off. He had come to defeat the great Fionn MacCoul and had been beaten by the hero's dwarf. He would never live it down! And for those who doubted such a story it was the custom of the locals to take them to the Eagle Stone and there on one of these stones alongside was clear to see – the marks of a giant thumb and forefinger.

st monenna

N THE 13TH AND 14TH CENTURIES Edinburgh Castle was referred to as The Castle of Maidens or in Latin, Castrum Puellarum. An old piece of local folklore told that this was because it was where the Pictish kings used to keep their princesses. The root of the name however appears to lie in its association with St Monenna. Like so many essentially mythical early Scottish saints Monenna is said to have come over from Ireland with a group of nine women. These were eight maidens, a widow and her son. In fact the name is probably linked to what seems to have been one of the most ancient and mysterious cults ever to have existed, that of the Nine Maidens. She had dedicated her life to spreading the Christian gospel and in time she had chapels dedicated to her on Edinburgh Castle Rock, Dumbarton Rock, Stirling Rock, and Dundonald in Ayrshire, the site, like the others, of an ancient fort or settlement.

Monenna was of course dedicated to serving her Christian God and therefore would have no association with men. However she was a beautiful young woman and had been sought after by many young, and not so young men in her native Ireland. She had of course spurned them all, having decided to devote her entire life to God. Having arrived in Galloway she and her

companions began to preach the word of the lord.
However it wasn't long before the beauty of this devout
young woman was noticed and commented on. Monenna
had set up her chapel on the western shores of Luce Bay
in the south-west of Scotland. A local chieftain, a young
and healthy man in his '20s, heard of this new arrival
and, coming to check on the reports of her beauty,
he saw her and fell in love with her at first sight.
He asked one of her companions to tell her he wanted
to speak to her and as she came to meet him he fell
on one knee, took her left hand in both his, and said,
'Fair Monenna I have never beheld one so lovely as you,
and I would like you to become my wife'.

Monenna pulled her hands away and stepped back.

'I have no interest in being any man's wife,' she said,
bowing her head, 'I have dedicated my life to serving
Christ. Now please leave.'

She turned on her heel and disappeared into the
small chapel.

However the young man was not easily put off
and over the next few weeks he kept coming back
to the chapel and attempting to speak to Monenna.
Her companions tried to keep him away but he would
not be put off. It was clear that he had set his heart on
making Monenna his wife.

Monenna herself prayed and prayed for guidance
and after one particularly stressful visit it came to her
what she must do. She called her nine companions to
her and said, 'Now you must follow me and trust me

completely. This man has made our stay here impossible and if we are all to fulfil our vows to God we must go and preach in some other place.'

She then led them down to the beach and onto a large rock that was half in and half out of the water.

'Now' she said, 'I want you all to pray with me,' and bowed her head. As the group of women prayed with bowed heads there on the rock, a wondrous thing happened. The rock began to float and within minutes it was floating away from the land. Right across the 30-mile wide Luce Bay the great rock floated with its precious cargo, eventually coming to shore at Farnes, now part of Glasserton parish and not far from the famous Isle of Whithorn where St Ninian had his church. Here they thought they would be safe from the attentions of the love-struck chieftain.

However the chieftain was a man of strong will and used to having his own way. Hearing of how Monenna and her companions had floated away on the tide he decided to follow her, miracle or no miracle. A couple of days after the group of women had landed, they began to build a simple wattle and daub church, plastering clay onto woven wooden hurdles, at a spot not far from where they had come to shore. They were all busy at their work when one of them called out to Monenna.

'Mistress look,' she shouted pointing to the north. 'He has come again.' There in the distance was the mounted figure of Monenna's suitor, accompanied by half-a dozen warriors.

The armed warriors rode up to the women and the chieftain dismounted. He came forward to Monenna and again getting down one knee he said. 'I respect your devotion, sweet Monenna but is it not true that the Lord has made us man and woman that we may populate the earth? I love you with all my heart and I promise that I will be a good and faithful husband to you, for is it not written that we should go forth and multiply? Please dear Monenna re-consider and be my wife.'

It was clear that he had taken advice from some priest or monk, and put a lot of thought into his speech and Monenna panicked. She thought she could never get away from this ardent would-be suitor and she turned on her heels and ran away from the shoreline. Her companions made to follow her but at a word from their chieftain the warriors ran between the maidens and the fleeing Monenna. The chieftain himself ran after her up a small rise towards a group of blackthorn trees. By now Monenna was shaking with fear, sure that in his obsession with her this young man was likely to take her by force. Reaching the copse of trees, and ignoring the thorns tearing at her clothes and her flesh Monenna clambered up the tallest of the blackthorn bushes and clung to a sturdy branch, dishevelled and bleeding. The young man came up to the clump of bushes.

'Oh Monenna, do not be afraid of me. I wish you no harm. I want only to make you happy and to live our lives as man and wife.'

As she heard him speak the fear left Monenna and

she felt herself grow very calm. She felt absolutely certain that whatever happened she would be fine, the Lord would protect her.

She looked down at the smiling man and asked him, 'What is it about me that you love so much that you must pursue me against my, and God's will.'

His smile grew broader as he replied, 'My lovely Monenna, ever since I first looked into your eyes I have been unable to think of nothing but you and my love for you. You have the most beautiful and tender eyes in the all the world, and they tell me you have a pure, sweet heart.'

'So it is my eyes that you love?' Monenna asked in a strangely calm and detached voice.

'Well, it's not just your eyes, but they are what caught my heart my love...'

His words dried up as he saw the young woman in the blackthorn bush reaching out to break off two long thorns. Whatever could she be doing?

'So it is my eyes that have laid the spell of love on you?' she said, and without a moment's hesitation, and looking at her suitor all the time, she stabbed the thorns into her eyes, twisted them and yanked her beautiful grey-green eyes clean from their sockets. With the blood pouring down her face she held the blood-dripping thorns with their grisly trophies towards him.

'Here you are. You can have my eyes. Now leave me alone.'

The poor man almost fainted, fell to his knees and

was violently sick. He realised now that there was no way he could ever make this woman his wife. She was clearly mad.

Stumbling, he turned away and headed back to where the others were, leaving Monenna, her sightless orbs trickling blood, sitting in the blackthorn. He went back to his companions, they all mounted their horses and rode off, never to bother Monenna again. Her companions came running up, all in state of shock, to help her from the tree.

'Worry not, maidens,' she said as her foot touched the ground. 'It is all God's will and all will be well, you will see.'

And she was right, for, due this remarkable testimony to her devotion to the cause of Christianity Monenna herself was the subject of one of God's miracles. She asked to be taken to the nearby well where she bathed her sight-less sockets and woke up the following day with her eyes and her sight restored.

In support of this tale there is the fact that the well, and many others that were dedicated to Monenna, were used by people who had troubles with their sight.

It is an interesting fact that when the site of St Margaret's Chapel, the oldest building in the Castle, was excavated in 1854, all the skeletons found buried there were female. Another story says that there was a nunnery here long, long ago but that the nuns had to be moved elsewhere because of the attentions of randy soldiers from the Castle. The other sites of dedications to St Monenna, like Stirling and Dumbarton Rock and Traprain Law, near Haddington in East Lothian (and visible from the castle) were all sites of great importance to the tribal peoples of first millennium Scotland and these dedications echo many other sites and stories that relate to groups of nine women, sometimes associated with single powerful females and sometimes on their own. One such group was Morgan and her eight sisters who were said to inhabit the sacred island of Avalon, where they took Arthur after his last battle with Modred at Camlaan.

the nine maidens and
the dragon

BOUT FIVE MILES NORTH of Dundee at the foot of the Sidlaws there is a Pictish symbol stone known as Martin's Stane. Such stones are widespread in eastern and northern Scotland and though many of them are from the post-Christian period, the earliest of them, known as Class I stones, have beautiful designs that hark back to the ancient beliefs of the tribal peoples before the first Christian missionaries came here in the fifth century. Martin's Stone, a later post-Christian Class II symbol stone, shows a serpent, a horseman and the strange creature known as the 'swimming elephant' or beastie. Both the serpent and the beastie were used on Class I stones. Above these three symbols, the bottom half of another horseman can be seen on a raised section which has been broken off. Although we can have no definitive idea of the real meaning or function of the beautiful and enigmatic Pictish symbol stones there is a tradition that gives a remarkable explanation of this one. A local rhyme goes;

'It was temptit at Pittempton
Draggelt at Ba'dragon
Stricken at Strikemartin
And killed at Martin's Stane.'

It seems that long ago there was a farmer who had
nine beautiful daughters. They lived at Pittempton
about two miles to the south of Martin's Stane.
The eldest was in love with a local lad called Martin.
One particularly hot day the farmer was working in
his fields and, feeling thirsty, he sent his eldest daughter
to the nearby well to fetch him a drink. After a while
when she hadn't returned he sent his next eldest after her.
When she too did not return, the farmer, getting thirstier
by the minute, sent all his daughters to the well one after
another. None returned.

Angry because he thought that his children were
playing a trick on him the farmer eventually stormed
off to the well himself. There a truly horrific sight met
his eyes. Wrapped around the well was a gigantic, scaly,
dragon-like creature with the dismembered bodies of his
lovely lasses scattered around it.

He let out a great cry of grief and horror and
everyone working in the nearby fields came running
at the noise, bringing their farm tools as weapons.
They were people used to having to fight off raiders
and most thought that they were being attacked by
people from another clan. We can only imagine their
horror when they responded to the cry and came
to the well to see that hideous beast and the bodies
of the nine young women. As they approached that
foul and heartrending sight the first among the crowd
was Martin, carrying a large tree branch he had picked
up to use as a club.

Seeing them coming the dragon lost interest in the girls' father, turned and slithered off to the north through the muddy hollow at Baldragon. Martin was hard on its heels. Running well ahead of the others, Martin caught up with the monster just as it was crossing the Dighty Water. The crowd roared, 'Strike Martin', and he dealt the beast a mighty blow with his club. A village now stands on this spot, nowadays known as Strathmartine but tradition says it used to be Strikemartin.

The blow seemed to do the beast no obvious harm, but it increased its speed and carried on northwards. After fetching some horses, Martin and a group of other young men, armed themselves with lances, or long spears, mounted up and chased after the fleeing creature. They caught up with it three miles to the north, just before it reached the Sidlaw hills, the hills of the Sidh, the fairy people. Once there it would have been much harder to trail and may well have escaped. However they managed to catch up and head the evil beast off just before it reached the sanctuary of the hills. Surrounding it in a circle they gradually closed in. The creature spat and fought using its tails and talons but it was heavily out-numbered and though they lost some horses, the men of Strathmartine managed to put an end to it, Martin himself giving it the coup de grace when he struck his spear into the black heart of that foul monster who had killed his beloved. And there on that spot, in commemoration of that dreadful day the people raised the Pictitsh symbols stone, the broken remains of which are still to be seen in the field to the left of the road just before it runs to run east parallel to the Sidlaw Hills. And they called it Martin's Stone in honour of the brave young man whose heart was broken that fateful day.

scotland's national flag

HROUGHOUT MUCH OF the seventh and eighth centuries the Picts had been involved in battles with the expanding kingdom of Northumbria. There had been bloody affrays in the Lothians and much further north, including the decisive Battle of Dunnichen, fought in 685. This was the battle that most probably preserved the independence of the Picts when under the leadership of Brudei mac Bile they virtually wiped out the great Anglian army of Ecgfrith, King of Northumbria. Today many people accept that this battle was fought at Dunnichen near Forfar and close to the famous Aberlemno Kirkyard Stone which depicts a battle between the Picts and the Angles, though there are those who think it was possibly in Fife or even much further north in Strathspey. There is one other battle involving the Picts and Northumbrians though, where there is no doubt about the location, or its importance in Scottish history.

This battle took place much later when once again the Northumbrians were on the march. Now in those far off days when we talk of kingdoms we don't mean that they were like modern nation states with clearly defined borders. Things were much more fluid back then and given the essentially tribal nature of much of British society back then it is even likely that many

of the battles we think of as dynastic were maybe just
as much to do with raiding for cattle and other goods
as they were about anything to do with kingship.
Be that as it may in 832 the Nothumbrians were once
again marching north through the Lothians. The king
of the Picts, Angus, realising that the Northumbrians
under their own king Athelstan were much more
numerous than any army he could put together,
had entered into an alliance with Eochaidh, king of the
Scots of Dalriada. Together they hoped their combined
forces could stop the Southrons in their tracks.
Both knew that if the Northumbrians defeated either
one of them it wouldn't be long before the other was
in deep trouble. Although the Picts and Scots had
often been at each other's throats over the centuries
they were in many cases related and several Scots
had actually been kings of the Picts before this.
Angus's own father Fergus was probably a Scot anyway
and it is likely that he and Eochaidh saw each other
as cousins. As Scotland's history clearly shows this
would not have stopped them fighting each other if
they thought it was worth their while but once again
it was clear that the Angles of Northumbria were
intent on taking over as much of Britain as they could.
Simply to survive, the Picts and Scots had to defeat them.
Both kings were aware that the Northumbrians would
have no intention of stopping at the Forth and that the
Anglian army would conquer all of Alba if they could.
So they decided to launch a preventative raid on the

Northumbrian troops that had already begun moving into the Lothians.

The combined armies of the Picts and the Scots marched south-eastward through the Lothians and down into the lands known as the Merse. Initially they met with success and the Northumbrians melted away before them. However it wasn't long before their scouts let them know that a massive army of Angles and Saxons was heading north led by Athelstan, a famed Northumbrian war-leader. Given the numbers that were approaching Angus and Eochaidh had little choice but to retreat northwards. However they also knew that they would have to turn and fight at some point or the Northumbrians would simply pursue them deep into their own territories. Angus was certain that he would not be able to turn the tables on Athelstan the way that Bridei had tricked Ecgfrith all those generations before. But both men knew there was little choice but to turn and fight at some point. So they were looking for a suitable ground to stand and fight when they came to the river Peffer which runs from near Haddington to the North Sea. In those far-off days before the countryside was drained for modern farming, the Peffer was a much bigger watercourse than it is today and the combined Pictish and Scottish forces decided to stand and fight at a ford across the river not far from East Linton.

The hope was that fighting at the ford would give them some advantage in the coming battle as only limited numbers of Northumbrians would be able to come at them at any one time. The site of the stand was in the area of Markle just to the north of the modern village of Athelstaneford, where the Peffer, which flows into the Firth of Forth at Aberlady, forms a wide valley. Being then wholly undrained, the Peffer presented a major obstacle to crossing, and the Picts and Scots camped near the modern farm of Prora -one of the field names there is still known as the Bloody Lands. Once more scouts were sent out to see where the Northumbrians were. The news that came back was bad, very bad. The much larger force of Northumbrians, with their Saxon allies, were approaching the Picts and Scots from three directions. The situation appeared hopeless. By now it was late in the day and the scouts reckoned that the invaders would be upon them at first light the next day.

The situation appeared hopeless but neither Angus nor Eochaidh were cowards. They would pray for guidance and go into battle like true warriors when the Northumbrians came upon them. So Angus led the assembled force in prayers, all of them kneeling in ranks before the two kings. As he finished his prayers Angus looked up into the clear blue sky. There, across most of the visible sky, was a great sign. It was a massive diagonal cross. Against the blue of the sky it could hardly be clearer.

'What is this sign?' he exclaimed.

At that one of the monks accompanying the armies came forward and said, 'That, Angus, is the shape of the cross on which the Blessed St Andrew, brother of the great Saint Peter, was martyred. I think he has sent us a sign.'

'If this be true,' said Angus raising to his feet and drawing his sword, 'it is perhaps then a sign of our victory and I will pledge this here and now. If we win the victory against these marauding Northumbrians tomorrow, we shall take this sign as a flag and we will make St Andrew our patron saint.'

The warriors nearby heard what the king had said and whispers spread throughout the ranks. There had been a sign from a great Christian martyr. Surely it meant that victory was assured. They all began to rise and look at the sky above. Realising that the sign was visible to all Angus turned and whispered to Eochadh. Both then raised their swords and addressed their warriors in their own tongues telling them of this great sign of victory that had come to them.

The next day the Northumbrian army came on the Picts and the Scots and the battle was hard. Just when it seemed that all would be lost once again the great cross appeared in the sky and the warriors of Angus and Eochaidh fought with renewed vigour as the great symbol caused fear and consternation amongst the Southron forces. The fighting was at its wildest and bloodiest at the crossing of the Peffer Burn where Athelstan himself fell, fighting like a true warrior to the very last and it was afterwards given the name of Athelstaneford because of his bravery.

When the battle was done at last and Angus and Eochaidh met amongst the piled corpses of the slain, both were convinced that divine intervention had helped them win this great victory even if it had cost them dearly in the number of warriors, friends and relatives that lay dead around the battlefield. The rump of the Northumbrians was heading back south and the great Athelstan had been defeated. Within 50 years of this great victory, the Picts and the Scots were finally united under Kenneth MacAlpin and, following in the vows made by his predecessors, he was pleased to declare St Andrew the patron saint of the new united country and to adopt as the national flag the white diagonal cross against a sky blue background that had so inspired the warriors of the Picts and Scots that distant day in the Lothians when it appeared in the sky to inspire them to a remarkable victory.

clans and culture

colonel anne

T IS AN ODD FACT that few women take centre stage in the stories that survive of the clans. They are usually present either as wives of central characters or occasionally as wise women who are either healers or have some visions of the future.

These latter are possibly some kind of folk memory of ancient priestesses which no doubt accounts for them sometimes being presented as witches, whether of the black or white variety. But there is one particular lady who stands out in the period of the '45, the Jacobite rebellion led by Bonnie prince Charlie. This is Anne Mackintosh – daughter of Farquharson of Invercauld. She married the chief of Clan Mackintosh and lived with him at Moy Hall, ten miles south east of Inverness. She was not long married and still only 20 when Prince Charlie arrived in Scotland. Now the clans were like the rest of British and Scottish society split over which side to support, the Hanoverians or the Jacobites. Anne's father was on the Hanoverian side but she herself was staunchly Jacobite, while her husband was an officer in the British Army. She however called out the clan for Charlie and there is a description of her at the head of her clansmen 'with a man's bonnet on her head, a tartan riding habit richly laced and a pair of pistols at her saddle bow.' Now she then might have ridden out for Moy Hal at the head of the clan but she was too sensible a woman to take on the command of the clan. As a woman she had no military experience. This was the responsibility of the clan Captain Alexander MacGillivary.

At the battle of Prestonpans where General Cope was so soundly beaten the Laird of Mackintosh was taken prisoner with his brother-in-law young Invercauld. They were in fact captured by a troop of scouts from Mackintosh's own clan and when he asked to be brought before a person of rank to formally surrender, they brought him to his wife. As he handed over his sword to her she said, 'Your servant, Captain,' to which he replied, 'Your Servant, Colonel.' She is also said by some to have been with the Mackintoshes at the Battle of Falkirk.

However the engagement she is best remembered for is one that took place not far from her home at Moy Hall.

It was in February 1746 that Prince Charlie, on his long retreat from England, came to Moy Hall 16 miles to the south east of Inverness. He arrived with a small detachment of troops to be welcomed by Anne and given traditional Highland hospitality. He had left a larger group of Highlanders under the command of Cameron Locheil a few miles to the south. These however numbered little more than 500 men.

Now up in Inverness Lord Loudon was in command of a Hanoverian force numbering over 1,500 men, quite a few of them having been brought in by MacLeod of Dunvegan. Amongst them were several who would far rather have been on the Prince's side and one of them

was MacCrimmon the hereditary piper to Macleod of
Dunvegan. Word came to Inverness from Grant of
Delachny that the Prince was at Moy Hall and that if
a strong force was sent out they would have little trouble
in capturing him. This was a very attractive proposition
for Loudon as apart from the kudos it would bring it
would effectively put an end to the rebellion if they could
capture the chief rebel himself!

So the combined force of government troops and
MacLeods set out for Moy from Inverness leaving a strong
guard on the gates of Inverness to prevent any word being
sent ahead. However the plans had been overheard by
a Mackintosh lass who was serving in the house where
Loudon had billeted himself and his general command.
Once the troops had left she ran to the nearby home of
the Dowager lady Mackintosh, Anne's mother-in-law,
and told her what was happening. Like her daughter-in-
law. Lady Mackintosh was Jacobite and realised that
something had to be done. She called a young lad of the
clan who worked for her called Lachlan and told him he
had to get out of the town and take word to Moy Hall
that the troops were on their way.

Now Lachlan Mackintosh was a lad in his early teens
who knew his way around Inverness and the hills between
the city and Moy Hall as well as anyone. It was an easy
task for him to sneak out of the town despite the guards
and to head off into the hills.

Lord Loudon's regiment and the contingent of
MacLeods were marching down the main road south and

Lachlan knew how dangerous it would be to try and pass them in the dark. They were liable to have a scout out ahead and behind the main body of troops, and the stars and the crescent moon were giving off some light. Still he would have to go some of the way on the road – going over the hills in darkness would take just too long. So he headed down the road keeping his eyes and ears open. He hadn't been going long and had just turned a bend onto a long exposed straight stretch of road, when he heard a noise behind him. It sounded like a detachment of horses following the government troops. They were coming down the road at a fair pace, considering the only light was that of the moon and stars. The young lad barley had enough time to throw himself into the roadside ditch before the horses came round the bend. Once they were past he dragged himself out of the muddy water and ran as fast as he could after them. He was sure he would hear when they caught up with the main detachment.

It was only a few minutes later when he heard the horses slow down and a command came faintly on the night air, 'Halt in the King's name. Who goes there?'

The horsemen had caught up with the troops and Lachlan at once turned to his left and headed into the hills. Keeping a couple of hundred yards off the road he made his way as quickly as he could. Soon he could see the troops and the faint light glinting of the shouldered muskets of Lord Loudon's Regiment. His way was hard but he was young and fit and he soon realised that though the soldiers had advance and rear guards set they didn't seem to have any roving patrols parallel to their main body. They were pinning their hopes on getting to Moy Hall quickly and surprising the Jacobites. But as quick as they marched they were no match for a young Highland laddie raised in these hills. Still he had to be careful and it took him a good while to catch up and pass the detachment of soldiers and clansmen. At last though he was well past them and could take to the road. Once he was back on the road he ran like a hare all the way to Moy Hall, stopping only to drink form roadside burns along the way. As he ran, heavy rain began to fall and in the distance he could hear the rumble of thunder.

By the time he got to Moy, ten long miles from the Highland capital, he was exhausted. The Jacobite troops had no outliers and the first guard he met was only a couple of hundred yards form the Hall overlooking Loch Moy. The first he knew of the guard was when a rough hand grabbed in from behind and he felt a dirk at his throat.

'Who are you and where are you going laddie?' a voice asked in Gaelic.

Replying in the same tongue he said, 'I am Lachlan Mackintosh. There are over a thousand troops coming down the road behind me. They know the Prince is at the Hall. I must tell Lady Anne.'

'Right, come along then,' said the Highlander releasing him and running alongside him as they ran to the sentry stationed at the door of the hall.

Within minutes all were awake and Lady Anne was questioning the bedraggled and exhausted young lad.

'How far are they behind Lachlan?' she asked gently. Outside the hall the prince and his men were already mounting their horses. They were heading back to join Lochiel's men and it seemed as if they would have to make a stand a few miles down the road. Anne Mackintosh however had a different plan.

'Well I think they will be more than half an hour yet,' the lad gasped, still trying to recover his breath! 'I ran most of the last few miles.'

'Well done Lachlann Mackintosh,' Anne said pressing him gently on the shoulder, 'this will not be forgotten.'

At that she went outside to say farewell to Prince Charlie who thanked her for her hospitality before heading off at a gallop with his small group of men.

'Right.' she said, 'how many men have we here?'

Looking around she realised the situation she was in. Apart form Lachlan, herself and the women servants most of the Mackintosh were still with the scattered detachments of the Jacobite army. There were only five men of fighting age there at the hall. Sending the women servants into the nearby woods to hide the Prince's baggage cart which had been left behind, she turned to a man ever after known as *Captein nan coig*, the captain of the five.

'Well, Dairmaid Fraser,' she smiled at the heavy-set middle-aged man before her, 'will you go and see what is coming our way.'

Standing there, a musket in his hand, a sword and pistols in his belt, Fraser bowed his head. 'Och we might just do a little more than that. Come on Lads.'

He turned on his heel, and ran off up the road followed by the other four men all armed with muskets, pistols and swords.

They ran off onto the moor land and at a spot on the moor where there was a bit of a hollow about two miles from Moy Hall, he stopped and laid his plans. There at *ciste chraig nan eoin,* the rocky hollow of the birds, he spread his men out in a line and told them what to do. They could not hope to halt a force of a thousand men but they could delay them and every minute they held them up the more chance that the Prince might be able to escape.

Minutes later they heard the sound of marching feet. The only other sound they could hear was the sound of horses' hooves hitting the rough road. By now the rain was falling in torrential bursts as the centre of the storm came nearer. Suddenly there was a great flash of lighting and ahead of them on the road the five men saw the approaching troops. All 1,500 of them. At their head, his pipes under is arm and his plaid over his head strode Donald Ban MacCrimmon, hereditary piper to MacLeod of Dunvegan. Again the lightning flashed but this time a shot rang out. MacCrimmon fell and all at once a volley of fire came from ahead. Voices shouted, 'to the left Mackintoshes,' and 'to the right Camerons'. The column halted. Cries of 'Ambush,' went up and some of the

troops began to turn back. Most of the MacLeods were at
the rear of the column and the government men began to
fall back on them causing confusion in the darkness.
And all the time the voices up ahead were shouting and
shots were ringing out. Loudon, near the head of his
troops was having trouble controlling his horse as men
milled around him. Suddenly some of them began to run
back towards Inverness! As they ran they stopped the
regular troops from forming up and pressing ahead.
Fraser and his men were running about, across roads
ahead shouting and shooting. It seemed as if there were at
least dozens, if not hundreds of Jacobites on the road
before the government troops. As some of them fled the
scene and the others were scattered, Loudon tried to rally
his troops. Up at the front of the detachment the sound of
pipes were heard. It was Duncan Ban MacCrimmon.
Aware he had been mortally wounded he was playing a
bright and lively tune that no one had ever heard before.
A cousin of his wife's crawled up to where he lay and sat
beside him while he played his last tune. Several months
later he got back to Skye and went to see Donald Ban's
widow. He told her of what had happened that fateful
night and when he mentioned Duncan's last tune, she
asked him to sing it. He was no piper but he could carry a
tune and so he sang it to her and she knew what it was.

'That's the tune he composed when he thought
MacLeod was taking them off to fight for the Prince,'
she told her cousin. Many years later she said that Duncan
had heard the Banshee and knew well that his time was

short which was why he had composed the wonderful tune called Cha till MachCrimein, Macrimmon No More, that pipers still play today.

Duncan breathed his last and his pipes groaned into silence. Loudon was still having trouble trying to rally his men. The increasingly heavy rain, thunder and lighting were spreading confusion – a confusion that was added to by the constant whizzing of musket balls coming from up ahead. With so many of his men streaming back towards Inverness and the rest unable to regroup he gave in and called for a bugler to sound the retreat.

Ever since then this skirmish has been known as the Rout of Moy and was the cause of many red faces when the government troops later found out just how many men Captain na coig had with him that night on the moors near Moy Hall. They had been routed by five men and the only casualty of the engagement was Donald Ban MacCrimmon.

This was not the last of Colonel Anne's adventures. After the dreadful slaughter of Drumossie Muir which is know as the Battle of Culloden, the Mackintoshes were, like many other Highland clans, at the mercy of the Red Army, as the government troops were known. Over two hundred Mackintoshes fell at Culloden and it wasn't long after that a marauding band of troopers came to Moy Hall. Colonel Anne was there with the local minister when the troops rode up. One of them, noticing the minister looking at his watch snatched it from his hand.

'Give that back,' said Anne, 'and I will give you a guinea.'

'Damn it you rebel bitch. You have money have you,' replied the soldier and grabbed her purse. This contained 50 guineas, which was all she had.

'If she has that she must have more,' shouted another of the English troops and grabbed her by the shoulders.

'That is all I have left,' said Anne with all the dignity she could muster.

'Is that right, you rebel whore,' the soldier shouted and unsheathing his bayonet stabbed her in the chest. As she fell there was the sound of approaching horses. It was in fact an official party sent to arrest Anne for her part in supporting the Jacobite cause but the soldiers who arrived first didn't wait to find out. They ran off in the opposite direction with their booty. The horsemen arrived on the scene led by one Sir Everard Faulkner, a minor Scottish laird who knew Colonel Anne. He arrived to find her lying on the ground in the arms of the minister blood seeping from the wound on her chest. Luckily it was a pretty superficial wound and she managed to tell Faulkner what had happened.

He was about to send some of his men to capture the assailants when Anne stopped him. Realising that if they were captured and court-martialled the influence Faulkner could easily lead to them being hanged and even though that might mean she could get her money back, she persuaded Faulkner not to send men after them.

'There has been enough blood shed around here

already,' she said before being carried in to Moy Hall. When she had recovered she was arrested and for a period of six weeks she was incarcerated at Inverness. However she was a lady and was released into the care of the Dowager Lady Mackintosh. Clearly the government representatives in Inverness had no idea of Anne's mother-in-law's role in the Rout of Moy!

After Culloden when things had died down a bit, even if the government felt it necessary to garrison almost the whole of the Scottish Highlands, she returned to live with Aeneas again at Moy Hall.

A couple of years later they were in London and attended a dance at which the Duke of Cumberland was present. Being told who she was, the Duke asked her to dance with him, having already told the band to play *Up and Waur them awa Willie*, a well known Hanoverian tune in the Scottish idiom. Colonel Anne graciously consented but when the tune was finished and the Duke bowed to her, she spoke.

'My Lord, would you care for another dance?' she asked. The Duke could hardly refuse even if this was not quite normal protocol and nodded his consent.

'Right then,' she said, offering him her hand and, turning towards the band called out 'play us *Auld Stewart's back again*, lads,' and proceeded into the dance with the furiously blushing Duke of Cumberland.

the macdonald hen chief

BACK IN THE DAYS of clan society there was a custom known as fostering. It mainly concerned the families of the chiefs as their sons would be sent off to be brought up within another family of the clan from childhood through to late adolescence. The result of this was that, effectively, they had two families; their own direct blood kin and their foster family. It was widely believed that foster brothers would be even more loyal to a future chief than to his own brothers. As an old Highland saying tells us, 'Kindred to twenty degrees, fosterage to a hundred.' It was an integral part of clan society and there are many stories of the enduring loyalty and support of foster-brothers to various chiefs. Fostering the son of a chief in clan society was not seen as duty but an honour and the families who fostered chiefs' sons were accorded great respect. In a society where there never was a great deal of physical wealth such respect was of inestimable value and there were always families keen to foster. However sometimes the fostering was done outside the clan and this had another purpose. It was intended to prevent possible feuding between the clans but sadly it didn't always work.

Now one of the best known instances of fostering going wrong was that of a man who has come to be known as Ronald Gallda (Stranger) MacDonald. He was sent off as a boy to be brought up amongst the Frasers who lived around Glenmoriston, to the north of the MacDonald lands. His father reckoned that by having him brought up amongst the Frasers the existing ties between the two clans would be strengthened and he and his people would never have to worry about being raided by the Frasers. But as the old saying tells us, 'there's many a slip twixt the cup and the lip.' Ronald was with his foster brothers on Fraser lands when news came that his father had died. Now although there was always an aspect of election for a new chief it had been decided long before that Ronald would succeed his father as head of the Clanranald MacDonalds. The whole clan accepted the situation. So it was that Ronald headed back to his own people and his ancestral home at Castle Tioram there to take on the role of chief of the MacDonalds. Here a great feast awaited him. The investiture of a new chief was an event of major importance and the whole clan had gathered to put on the best possible show for Ronald. When he arrived on the flatland before Castle Tioram there was what appeared to be a small herd of cattle being roasted on spits over fires, while other fires were roasting whole deer from the hill. The MacDonald clanfolk had brought mountains of fresh-baked bread and great bowls of butter and cheese. And there was plenty ale and whisky, with more than a few bottles of good French claret. It was a veritable cornucopia of all the best and finest food that the clan lands could provide and everyone was in a great state of excitement. They had had the funeral of the old chief with all due solemnity but now was the time for celebration.

Ronald arrived with all of his Fraser foster-brothers, having been met at the edge of the Clanranald clan lands by his younger brothers and his uncles, all on horseback as he and the Frasers were. As they rode into the field where the feast had been laid out, Ronald looked around him and said, 'You know, you shouldn't have gone to this much trouble and laid on all this. A few hens would have done just as well.' This remark was met by a deadly silence and as he looked around with a puzzled expression on his face he began to realise something had gone wrong, very wrong. Whispers were running through the assembled MacDonalds and all signs of celebration disappeared as the entire crowd fell silent. Ronald looked at his brothers and uncles. All were staring grim-faced at him and he realised that several of them had drawn their swords. From somewhere in the assembled crowd he heard a voice say, 'We want nothing to do with a hen-chief, this man is not for us.' Another voice spoke, 'Ay he has been brought up too close to the lowlands and has forgotten who he is.' He looked to his foster-brothers but they seemed to be as perplexed as he was. And then one of his uncles spoke, 'We will be taking you back to the border Ronald Gallda, you are not fit to be our chief.'

It was a sombre band of men that rode back to the border of Clanranald territory. Ronald's brothers and uncles were accompanied by a couple of dozen heavily armed MacDonalds. At the border of the clan lands, they told him to go and return no more. He had shamed himself and the entire clan. Some thought that being brought up by the Frasers, he had forgotten his roots, but for the MacDonalds what he had done was unforgiveable. The investiture of a chief wasn't about the individual, it was for the whole clan. This was an ancient sacred rite to re-assert the ties between all the people claiming a common ancestry from Ranald, son of the Lord of the Isles. It was also of considerable importance that the whole clan should enjoy the rare and much appreciated feasting and of celebrations that accompanied such an event. And as the chief he should have been more aware of that than anyone. And from that day on Ronald Gallda has gone down in tradition as the Hen Chief of the MacDonalds, a fine joke for their enemies and a stain on the honour of his clan. One of his brothers was appointed to be chief in his place. But this was not the end of the affair.

Ronald Gallda's father's plan for peace between Clanranald and the Frasers ended up achieving the opposite effect. The MacDonalds were so incensed at Ronald's actions, blaming the Fraser's for subverting their chief's idea of history and tradition, that they called on the Camerons to join them in a raid on Fraser's land. It was considered that Lovat, the head of the Frasers, had failed in his fostering responsibilities and that all the Frasers should be made to pay for this insult.

This raid, in turn, set off a whole series of reprisals and on 15 July 1544 by the shores of Loch Lochy, the

MacDonalds and the Frasers, each accompanied by
warriors from allied clans, met in a famous and bloody
battle called *Blar na Leinne*, the Battle of the Shirts, and
in it Ronald Gallda laid down his life trying to regain
what he thought was rightfully his, the chieftainship of the
Clanranald MacDonalds. It took the Frasers many years
to recover form the disaster that befell them that day
because of their support for the Hen-Chief of the
MacDonalds.

son of the carpenter

HIGHLAND SOCIETY IN the Middle Ages was structured round the clan system. Now the clans were the direct descendants of the tribal people, the Picts, the Scots, and the Norsemen, all of whom had lived in Scotland in the earlier centuries and like them the clans were basically warrior peoples. They lived in close-knit family groups, usually no more than half a dozen families together, and like their forefathers, they reckoned their wealth and prosperity in terms of the cattle they owned. It was a hard but healthy life, essentially self-sufficient farming but with enough of a surplus now and again to allow for the bringing in of luxuries, like fine weapons and expensive cloth. The chiefs were often well-educated and all of the clanspeople had a fabulously rich tradition of story and song inherited from their ancestors, of whom they were extremely proud. Generally they called themselves after a famous ancestor who had founded their tribe or clan in the far past and many such ancestors had stories told of how they had got their name in the first place.

One such tale concerns the MacIntyres, a clan whom, for many generations, provided the hereditary pipers to the MacDonalds of Clanranald and the Menzie clans. Some of them also had an ongoing relationship with the MacDonalds' hereditary enemies the Campbells. This gave

rise to the strange situation where they had the right to
the Clan Donald badge, the heath plant, and the clan
Campbell war-cry, *Cruachan*! Traditionally they lived in
the lands around Glen Noe and Loch Etive in the far west
and, like many of the western clans, claimed to be of
Norse or mixed Norse-Gael ancestry. The name itself
means the son of the Carpenter and there are different
versions of who this carpenter originally was. Some
versions of the story say he was a nephew of Somerled,
the very first Lord of the Isles, who saved his uncle's ship
from sinking while others tell a different story.

That particular story tells us that the first of the
MacIntyres was originally a MacDonald, either from
Skye or the nearby mainland. The MacDonalds were the
biggest of all the clans, being split up into many different
sub-clans and living over a very wide geographical area.
Like all of the men of his clan, this MacDonald was as
accustomed to travelling on water as he was on land
and spent much of his life in his small boat off the coast.
However, somehow he broke the laws of his kin in a
serious fashion. The story does not tell us just what
his misdeed was but we can be sure that it was a serious
breach of clan law. In fact so bad was his misdeed that
he was towed a long way out to sea in an old leaky boat
and cast adrift. Before his companions, all of them his
blood-relations, left him they removed the bung from
the hole in the bottom of the boat. It could only be a
matter of time before the boat filled up with water and he
would be alone in the water. His companions raised the

sail in their own boat and taking off into the onshore wind, were soon were a good way off.

From where he had been abandoned the coast was below the horizon. He would in all probability drown long before he could hope to swim ashore. His situation appeared hopeless but where there is life there is hope he thought to himself. So he stuck the thumb of his left hand in the bung-hole of the boat to stop any more water coming in and bailed out as much of the water as he could with his right hand. He had no water, no food and no way of directing his boat. All he could do was drift at the mercy of the sea but stubbornly he clung to the thought that he might get lucky.

Once he had managed to get rid of some of the water in the boat it was clear that his situation wasn't getting any worse though he was aware, as all the people of the west coast were, that the weather could change very quickly. If a squall came up he would be finished. But he refused to despair. Luckily the sea remained calm and the wind stayed relatively light, blowing from the shore. It might only have been a light breeze but it was still slowly taking him ever farther from the shore and potential safety. He kept scanning the horizon every few minutes and after a couple of hours he saw a sail further out to sea. It seemed to be heading in towards the shore. He had to attract their attention but he was crouched down in the bottom of the boat held there by his thumb. If he pulled out his thumb and the boat filled with water and they didn't see him, he would be truly finished. But if he didn't wave and attract their attention he would be no better off than he now was. The chances of them spotting this old boat which lay quite low in the water were very slim indeed. He had to do something. Luckily, he had managed to hold on to his *sgian dubh,* the wee black knife that every Highlander, carried when he had been manhandled into the boat. He knew what he had to do. With no hesitation he took the knife in his right hand and slashed right through the base of his left thumb. Stopping only to rip a piece off his plaid to staunch the bleeding, he then whipped off his plaid and whirled it round and round his and shouted at the top of his voice. It wasn't long before he was spotted from the other boat.

The crew of the other boat, a considerably larger vessel, changed course and came to rescue him. They were men of another clan and when they saw just how he had managed to bung the boat's hole they said that it was as fine a piece of carpentry work as they had ever seen. They then took him to their own lands further up the coast where they did what they could to treat his wound. Once the word went round the community of what he had done he was known to one and all as *an T-saoir*, the Carpenter, and so his descendants became the MacIntyres.

a GRAND ARCHER

OW MALCOLM CANMORE was a great king it is said. Not only did he rule wisely within the borders of Alba but he was known throughout Europe. Maybe because of his wife, the saintly Margaret, who was of mixed English and Hungarian descent. Now kings have the habit of giving each other gifts as tokens of friendship though sometimes it must be said such gifts were more in the way of distractions while devious plots were being laid, such is the nature of kings. Although today such behaviour is more the remit of politicians. However one European king had given Malcolm a present of something that had never been seen, or heard of, in Scotland before. The story tells us it was a great beast the local people considered to be akin to a frog or a toad but from what we can tell was probably a crocodile. Whatever the beast was it had a fearsome appetite and once the king had installed it on *Eilean na Peiste*, the isle of the beast in the River Don, he set about arranging for it to be fed. Such was its appetite that he placed a tax of one animal per croft per year on the countryside. Now this was a swinging tax indeed but for the widow MacLeod it spelt disaster. She only had the one cow and the milk from it combined with her careful husbandry of her garden kept her alive. She had a son who helped her

out but he had a wife and a baby of his own to feed
and the widow was a fiercely independent woman. She
was also possessed of a biting tongue.

One day just after the announcement of the tax
had been made her son came to visit. 'You claim to be
of the blood of Torquil of the Eagles,' she spat at her son,
reminding him of the eponymous founder of their clan,
'but there is no blood of the MacLeods in your veins,
just water. You sit there by my fire while that Southron
king takes the very food form my mouth. Call yourself
a MacLeod warrior. Ochone, ochone what is to become
of me?'

MacLeod sat there silent under this tirade. Sure
enough he realised the situation and that his mother was
right in what she was saying. What right has this
Southron to come into their country and take the very
food from the mouth of the poor? He sat there saying
nothing as his mother ranted and raged until, at last, he
went off into the night, her curses following him like a
rabid dog. However he knew what he was about to do.
Returning home to his own house he quietly let himself in
and listening to make sure his wife and child were sleeping
he went to the place in the eaves where he kept is bow
and quiver full of arrows. Like all men of his time he was
a fully trained warrior but he was known to be far and
away the best archer for miles around. Stories were told
that he could hit the eye of a fly at 40 paces and bring
down a 12 point stag from half a mile away with his bow.
He knew these stories to be over the top but was sure

of his skills, and for what he intended he needed to be. Carefully unstringing the bow he wrapped the bowstring in a greased cloth before putting it inside a well-greased leather pouch, which he slipped next to his skin inside his shirt. Then he headed off into the night closing the door softly behind him.

He slipped through the night down to the banks of the river opposite Eilean na Peiste and lowered himself into the freezing cold waters with as little noise as possible. With his quiver over his back and his bow in his teeth he swam swiftly out to the island. Once there he pulled himself ashore and quickly pulling the pouch with the still dry bow-string in it, he restrung his bow. He took two arrows from his quiver, notching one to the bowstring and gripping the other between his teeth. Then he began to stealthily move along the island which was no more than 50 yards long and about 20 to 30 wide. He smelt the animal before he saw it. Then he heard it move and dropping to one knee in the faint moonlight he saw a great gleaming pair of eyes looking straight at him through the underbrush. Quick as a flash he sighted, drew and fired. His arrow flew straight into the left eye and a great roar erupted as the beast lurched back and fell over on its side. He had got it with his first shot.

The noise however had awakened the king's men who were guarding the beast on the banks of the river and suddenly both banks were lined with armed men holding torches aloft. Boats were launched east and west of the island and MacLeod realised that escape was impossible. Still he had done what he intended and his mother would have food for the winter. As to what would now happen to his wife and child he dared not think.

MacLeod was taken prisoner and held in the dungeon of a nearby castle till a few days later when the king had arranged to hold a Justice meeting on the nearby Gallows Hill. When MacLeod was brought before him the king was in no mood for mercy.

'You insolent pup. That creature was a royal gift from a great king from many hundreds of miles away over the sea and you thought you could just kill it as if it were one of your Highland wolves. Well you can think of how clever that was as you hang. String him up,' he said snapping his fingers at a nearby officer of his guard.

'Ah, sire can I have a word,' a voice came form his left side. It was Alan Durward, a close and trusted friend.

'What is it?' asked the king holding his hand up as the officer stepped forward to take MacLeod off to the great gallows set up just a few paces away.

'Well, you see this MacLeod is just the best archer we have in the district and we have been relying on him for training up the young lads. And you know you were saying yourself just recently that we have need of more archers, sire' Durward said gently. The king sat still looking at MacLeod, his hands tied behind his back and held firmly by two of the guard. The young man looked straight back at him, head held high. Just then there was a commotion in the crowd nearby and a young woman, clutching an infant to her breast burst form the assembled people.

She ran forward and threw herself at the king's feet.

'Oh sire, please spare him. He is all I and my son and his poor old mother have in all the world, He is a dear, dear man, please sire...' and she burst into tears as her husband looked grimly on.

The king sat still for another minute then he spoke. 'Here is my judgement. You MacLeod are an archer of some repute it seems. So guards take his wife and child over the other side of the river and place a peat on her head. If you can shoot the peat off her head without harming either of them MacLeod, your life shall be spared,' and the king smiled, a wee, grim smile. The watching crowd sucked in their breath. The river here was only 20 or 30 yards wide but from her position on the hill the shot was more than a hundred yards.

So the young woman and her child were taken across the river in a boat and a peat was placed on her head. She gathered all her strength and stood as straight and as still as she could. Then MacLeod's bow and quiver were brought and at a nod from the king his bonds were cut. He reached out for his bow and flexed it a couple of times. The he reached to the quiver and took an arrow which he placed between his teeth before taking another arrow and nocking it to the bowstring. The entire crowd fell silent.

MacLeod raised his bow and just as he sighted the tiny peat on his wife's head, his hands began to shake.

There was a great sigh from the crowd as he lowered the bow. The King smiled. Again MacLeod lifted the bow but yet again his hand shook. Again there was a great sigh form the crowd and the king smiled wider. So this great archer was not up to the challenge. Well, he thought, he will just have to hang. He was just about to raise his hand and give the order when MacLeod whipped up the bow, sighted and fired quicker than seemed possible. The arrow flew across the river and cleanly took the peat of his wife's head. The entire crowd erupted into cheering and relieved of the bow and arrow MacLeod was brought to face the king.

'Well MacLeod, you have shown your skill with the bow right enough and as I have said you shall be spared. But tell me, what was the second arrow for?' he asked quizzically.

'That sire, was for you if I missed or harmed my wife or son,' the young man spoke loud and clear and there was great indrawing of breath from all the lords and soldiers around the king. How dare any man speak to the king like that.

'Well,' said the king, 'I can see you are a brave and honest man, and I daresay you might have managed to kill me despite the presence of my guard. I have need of men like you. Will you become one of my guard and swear to protect and serve me?'

MacLeod looked long and hard at the king. There was absolute silence as all waited to hear what he would say.

'I am afraid I must refuse the honour your majesty.

After what you put me and my family through here today I could not swear to be as loyal as you would require,' and as he said this, for the first time he bowed his head to the king. All around were stunned. This man had been given his life back and now he was throwing the honour of being one of the king's guard right back in the king's face. Surely he must hang now!

Suddenly the king laughed. 'I see they breed their men tough up here right enough. You are as hardy a man as I have met in my life. You can go free but from now on by order of the king you shall be called Hardy.' And from that day on it was as the king said and in time the sons of the man born MacLeod became known as MacHardies.

mαcnαʙ αnꝺ the
sheriff's officer

OW IN THE OLD DAYS when chiefs were
still chiefs and the leaders of their clans,
before they had transmogrified into that
pale imitation of English gentry, the lairds,
there were more than a few sharp characters amongst
them. Being as they were heirs to centuries of self-
sufficiency in economic terms, some of them were none
too responsible when it came to money. After all hadn't
their ancestors been living off the land since the time of
the Flood? Some of them it would have to be admitted
were, as they say, a bit fly, and living much of their time
on the ancestral lands in the Highlands they were more
than capable of running up a fair amount of debt when
they did venture down to Edinburgh or even London.
One such was MacNab. On one trip to the capital he
had ordered a vast amount of good claret and brandy
to be delivered back up to his ancestral home then had
gone off on a tour of Edinburgh's finest emporia.
The upshot was he bought a very expensive pair of
customised pistols, several top class suits of clothing
in the Highland style and four or five pairs of boots.
He then headed off back to the mountains and the
glens and the bills were sent out in due course.
Nothing happened. A few weeks after that the city

merchants who had catered to MacNab's expensive tastes sent out a further round of bills for goods and services rendered. Nothing happened. Now as he had spent a great deal of money which he apparently didn't have the various affronted shopkeepers and artisans, considerably out of pocket, got together to try and sort the matter out. It was obvious to them that this Highland brigand had absolutely no intention of settling his debts. This was an affront to their pockets as much if not more than to their combined sense of propriety. MacNab's sense of propriety, such as it was, had developed from his ancestors, all of whom had been making predatory raids on other clans and occasionally the Lowlands for centuries so he could be said to be behaving in a time-honoured manner. Either way he wasn't much bothered.

The situation continued for a while and at last the Edinburgh merchants lost patience. They decided to set the law on MacNab. Accordingly they hired a lawyer, swore out the necessary affidavits and a sheriff's officer was sent to the MacNab ancestral lands to serve a writ on himself.

Now by this time the Highlands were supposedly pacified and the sheriff's officer with a legal writ in his possession was confident that he would have little or no trouble, after all hadn't he been assured that MacNab was a gentleman? However a Highland gentleman and a Lowland gentleman were not exactly the same thing.

When he reached MacNab's home, a fortified tower house with a stunning view over the beautiful River

Lochy, the officer was met at the door by the MacNab himself.

'Good afternoon,' said the chief taking the man by the hand and shaking it forcefully. 'Welcome to the land of my fathers, it is lovely isn't it?'

Without giving the man a chance to reply MacNab went on 'It has long been the tradition hereabouts for a visitor to have a drink on arrival. You will take a dram will you not?'

The officer didn't have a chance to refuse for one of MacNab's clansmen was immediately at his elbow pressing a large bumper of whisky into his hand.

'A toast,' cried MacNab, 'Here's to health wealth and prosperity for all of Scotland.'

And saying this he downed in one the contents of the glass he was holding in his own hand. The bemused Lowlander felt he had no choice but to do the same. So he tossed off the full glass of whisky in one. The effects were instantaneous. His cheeks flushed, a sweat broke out on his brow and it was with some difficulty that he managed not to cough.

'Well done,' said his host signalling to his henchman to re-fill both their glasses. This done he immediately downed the second glass and the sheriff's officer followed suit.

'Come on in, come on in, a thousand welcomes to my humble home, you will stay the night wont you?' said MacNab, ushering the bemused man into the house.

The sheriff's officer was about to state his business

at this point but MacNab just carried on talking as he
led his guest into the house. The poor man couldn't get
a word in edgeways and before having him shown to
his room MacNab called for two more large bumpers
of whisky. Now the sheriff's officer was an Edinburgh
man and was well used to drinking a significant amount
of claret but he was not used to the *uisge beatha*.
And truth to tell it was the very best of the amber nectar,
treasturring, the triple distilled favourite of the Highlander
and to say it had a kick would be like suggesting Ben
Nevis is a wee hill. So after three, admittedly large
glasses of this delightful liquid he had a bit of a glow on.
Now he was a man of some experience and reckoned
that he knew what MacNab was doing, he was trying
to get him drunk. Very well he would play along and
simply hand over the writ in the morning before he left.

Telling him he would see him at dinner time MacNab
went off and the officer was shown to his rather spartan
room. There was a bed, a big old chest, a table and a
chair. And on the table there was another bottle of whisky.
Wisely, he thought, the officer decided against taking more
of the amber nectar before the evening meal. He thought
he would just lie down for a little, and promptly fell
asleep. He was awakened a while later to be told that
dinner was about to be served and went down to join
his host in the big hall of the tower. Here he was regaled
with a meal of salmon and roast venison accompanied,
of course, by more and more whisky. There was a man
standing at this elbow and every time he drank his whisky

his glass was refilled. MacNab too had a man with a bottle standing at his elbow but the officer did not realise that this was full of water, well half full, the rest being whisky of course. So whisky after whisky was drunk and a great deal of food taken as the evening wore on. It didn't take long for the officer to begin to drift off to sleep in his chair. While he was dozing MacNab gave a signal to one of his clansmen who went off to do what had already been arranged.

Some time later the sheriff's officer was awakened and shown to his bed. In truth he was half carried but through it all he thought he had held out well and would sort things out in the morning.

It was the middle of the morning and MacNab was sitting by the fire in his own great hall when the door burst open. There stood his guest, ashen-faced and trembling.

'My good lad, what ever is wrong with you?' asked MacNab rising from his chair and going to him.

The man looked at him with his eyes almost popping from his head. 'Wha...wha... what is that outside my window?" he blurted out.

'Outside your window?' asked MacNab acting puzzled.

'Yes outside my, my window, hanging from that tree,' stuttered the Lowlander.

'Och that,' laughed MacNab, 'that's just a man they sent up here from Edinburgh a few days ago with some kind of summons for me.'

At this the sheriff's officer went even whiter and ran

from the room. He barely reached the front door before he was violently sick.

MacNab followed him to the door, where the man turned and said. 'I am s...s...sorry but I have some people to see, at once,' and headed off not even waiting for his breakfast. MacNab wandered round to the back of the tower and looked up at the straw man hanging from the tree and laughed, before heading back indoors for what he thought was a well-deserved dram.

the silver buttons

I T WAS 1746 AND Willie Mearns was 12 years old.
He lived with his mother and two little sisters at
Brocklas in Glen Clova, a two-roomed stone-built
house overlooking a steep descent to the river South
Esk. The year before he had stood at the Milton of
Clova at the head of the glen and watched his father
march off with the 800 men raised by David Ogilvy to
join the Jacobite Army. A few months later the dreadful
news of his father's death at Prestonpans had arrived,
and Willie was now the man of the house – with
responsibility for his mother and two wee sisters. He was
only in his early teens but already he was a powerfully
built lad, showing the signs of the big powerful man he
was to grow into. As he tended the small flock of sheep
the family had on the slopes of the hill called The Aud,
he often found himself in tears remembering his father's
last words to him.

'Mind now Willie, look after your mum and the girls
till I come back. It will be a grand day then with a new
king and better times for all of us.'

Much of the time he was downcast and had no one he
could speak to, so when Ogilvy's regiment came back to
same spot in the glen to disband in 1746, he watched
from a distance, angry that his father had seemed to have

died in vain. He had been caught up in the excitement of the army being raised for the young Prince, but now he was just angry and confused. However, he knew that his father had been happy to go out to join the Prince's army and his real hatred was reserved for the Redcoats – the government soldiers who had come into the glen a week or so after the Regiment had disbanded. They had looted and pillaged most of the glen. Luckily, from Brocklas on the other side of the river from the road up the glen, the Mearns family had seen what was happening and had managed to drive their sheep and two cows up out of sight of the marauding troops before they arrived. Still, they had lost precious goods when the soldiers stormed through their home.

Willie and his sisters could only watch from the hills above as the soldiers ransacked the house. When a soldier knocked his mother to the ground he began to run down the hill, shouting to his sisters to mind the beasts but by the time he got there his mother was sitting alone at the front door, telling him 'Never mind, Willie I am all right.' All that day, smoke rose from houses up and down the glen as the troops set fire to haystacks, barns and houses.

The next day Willie watched the troops march back out of the glen some pushing carts laden with what they had looted, followed by horse-drawn carts piled high with booty, much of which was of little use to them and soon to be discarded. Willie's heart raced and his head pounded with the anger he felt, but what could a 12-year-old laddie do against a hundred professional soldiers? Soldiers, he spat, they were nothing but bandits and thieves.

Within a few days though, Willie found there was something he could do. He was out on the Hill of Craigthran near the headwaters of the Burn of Cuillt when he saw something moving in a gorse bush at the side of the burn. At first he thought it was just a stoat or a weasel, but as he looked closer he saw that what had moved was an arm. Somebody was hiding in the gorse bushes. It could only be a rebel.

Now Willie was bright enough to approach the man carefully. If it was rebel, and it had to be, the man would be armed and quite likely ready to shoot anyone he saw as a threat. Cautiously he approached the bush and quietly said. 'Hello?'

'Who is there?' came the reply and Willie saw a movement, realising by the movement in the bushes that the man had pointed a pistol in his direction. 'I am a friend,' Willie said quickly, 'my name is Willie and my father died for the Prince at Prestonpans.'

At that point the man groaned and Willie saw the pistol drop. He came forward and parted the bushes. There, lying on the ground was an unshaven, well-dressed man in a jacket, waistcoat and trews, and on the left side of his jacket an ominous dark, wet patch. Willie knew right off that the man was badly wounded.

'Here,' he said knelling by the man and pulling out his leather water bottle from the knapsack he carried with him, 'take a drink.'

The man reached for the bottle with his right arm and took it, raised it to his lips and gulped furiously. He then gave a cough and fell back, letting the bottle fall. As he lay there he looked directly at Willie for the first time and gave a slight smile.

'Well, Willie, will ye help me?' He asked.

'I will do whatever I can,' said the lad. 'I have some bread and cheese here in my bag. Can you eat?'

The man nodded, and Willie gave him some bread and cheese which he gobbled down furiously. It was clear he had not eaten in some time. Once he had eaten he fell back as if tired out with the effort, and his eyelids fluttered as if he would fall asleep. That was not a good idea Willie thought and he said to the semi-comatose stranger, 'Look, can you move? My home is less than two miles off and I can give you a hand. My mother will be able to take a look at your wound but if you stay here...'

The man looked him in the eye, 'Are there any Redcoats about?'

'There's a corporal and four men, but they are at the head of the glen and they never come down this far,' the young lad replied. 'If we wait till the gloaming and are careful, we can keep out if sight of the road for most of the way. Can you manage it?'

'It seems I have no real choice,' replied the man with a grim smile.

He was obviously in great pain and once the day had begun to fade it was a hard job for Willie to help him down the hillside. Most of the time he was virtually carrying the man. By the time they were close to Brocklas, the man's face was deathly white and his breath was coming in great laboured gasps. Willie was also aware that the damp patch on his left side was spreading. As they neared the house, one of Willie's sisters saw them coming and ran indoors to fetch her mother. She came running up the hill to give Willie a hand to carry the stranger the last couple of hundred yards to the house. By now the last of the gloaming was on them and it would soon be dark. Once at the house, they carried him in and laid him on the simple box bed in the main room. As they laid him down he gave a groan and passed out.

Mrs Mearns looked at her son with a look he had never seen before, but she only said, 'Fetch me hot water and get an old sheet from the kist, Willie. Girls, light a candle.'

Carefully in the soft light of the candles she cut the man's jacket away and undid his blood-soaked waistcoat. Under it his fine linen shirt was totally soaked with blood, much of it congealed but there was still some of it seeping through. She cut away the shirt to expose a hole in the man's side the size of a musket ball. Lifting him as gently as she could, she pulled the shirt from his back. There was a bigger hole which was oozing blood from round a half-formed scab.

'He's lucky,' she said, 'the ball went straight through. We can probably save him.'

So she cleaned and bandaged the wound and when she was done she draped a blanket over the man who had by now fallen into a deep, troubled sleep.

'Now girls,' she said, 'nobody is to hear we have this visitor, it is to be our secret and tomorrow and the days after I want you to keep an eye out for anyone coming to the house. If anyone does come you are to run and tell me. Do you understand?'

The two young lasses, Kirsty who was nine and Isabel eight, nodded. They had seen enough trouble in their short lives to know that keeping this man's presence a secret was important

'All right then, have your supper and off to bed with the pair of you,' she said as she took off the clothes of the man in the bed. She proceeded to wash them in the big tub that sat at the front door before hanging them inside the house, all the time deep in thought and saying nothing to her son. He spent much of the time looking at the stranger in the bed and thinking of his father. Later, though, the pair of them talked deep into the night. Before going to sleep Willie hid the man's clothing and his pistol in a hollow tree on the hillside above the house.

For the next few days, the girls kept an eye out as the man was fed with soup. By the second day, he was sitting up and managed to eat some lamb stew. It turned out he was from Edinburgh, a bookseller to trade, but his family were Episcopalians and he had headed west as soon as he had heard the Prince was raising his standard. After the disaster of Culloden, he had been heading south through Glen Esk towards Dundee where he had some friends, when he had been seen by a patrol and shot. He had tumbled down the bed of a stream and had managed to crawl nearly ten miles to where Willie found him.

For nearly a fortnight the Mearns family took care of their visitor, and when at last he was ready to leave, he took a *sgian dubh* from inside his jacket and cut the 12 silver buttons off his waistcoat.

'These are for you,' he said giving six to Mrs Mearns and the other six to Willie, 'it is little enough for what you have done for me but you can sell these and live a little better in these hard times.'

Despite their protests that they were only giving him the necessary hospitality of tradition, he insisted they take the silver buttons. Taking Mrs Mearns by the hand, he smiled and said, 'If I had been found, you and Willie would have been jailed at the very least and well you know it. I am forever in your debt.'

And a hundred years later when Granny Mearns told the story to her grandchildren, she would pull out the last three of the silver buttons to show how true the story was.

the clean shaven minister

A LOT HAS BEEN SAID, sung and written about the glorious beauty of Scotland over the centuries. Painters and poets have thrilled at the exquisite and dramatic scenery that can be found in so many different parts of this wonderful land. A flavour of how Scots themselves see the land can be seen in the weel-kennt tale of God and St Peter. God called Peter in one day when he was creating the earth and said, 'Look Pete, this is wee cracker of a country I'm making here. It has beautiful, soaring mountains, sheltered lovely glens, the purest water anywhere on earth and air so pure you could bottle and sell it. The mountains are full of beautiful red deer, the rivers with salmon and in the lowlands there is lush, rich grass for all sorts of livestock.'

'I presume you'll be putting people in here,' queried Peter.

'Oh aye,' said God. 'They will be a proud, adventurous, creative and friendly lot I reckon.'

'But don't you think you're spoiling them a bit with all this?' Asked the Big Fisherman.

'Och just you wait till you see their neighbours,' came the reply.

Now it is true that we Scots do like to take pot-shots at the English now and again but they are nothing compared to how the Glaswegians and Edinburghers talk of each other so just grin and bear it if you are from the lesser part of this fine island.

However to offset the undoubted majesty of the country there is of course the weather. The depressing months of little daylight, filled with what seems an endless variety of permutations of cold, wind, sleet, rain and snow, some years seems to last forever. And along with this general inclemency we have various forms of illness. We have considered the Buchan method of how to deal with the sniffles but here is a variation on the story of the need to defend one's body against the incursions of the cold, flu and other nasties.

It took place over a hundred years ago, at a time when virtually everybody in all the rural parishes of Scotland was a regular churchgoer. It is all too easy to paint this as a fanaticism but it cannot be denied that the Kirk held communities together in ways we now see was beneficial indeed. The central importance of the Kirk to community life was obvious but it brought some limitations, particularly to ministers. Now as we have seen already, there were more than a few ministers who well understood that whisky was itself one of God's blessings, but this was not a universally held point of view.

There was once a minister, himself a McDrouthy, who had strayed from the well-worn path of his ancestors and entered the Kirk who was not on of those who fulminated excessively against the demon drink. He had, on occasion, when propriety suggested it taken a drink or two but by the standards of his forebears was abstemiousness personified. At the time of the story he was a man in his 40s, still single, and had a house-keeper called Janet who was truly ancient. Nobody knew exactly how old Janet was but she had 'done' for three previous ministers in the same manse and had a particular view of the universe. This was a narrow-mined view that was matched only by her pride in her own station as housekeeper to the minister–though she would have been mortified to have had her feelings described as pride. That was a sin! And Janet was a body who was against sin in all its forms. However she was vey efficient house-keeper and a first-class, if somewhat pedestrian, cook. The minister appreciated her skills and was careful never to upset her.

Now one time the minister had come down with a nasty dose of the sniffles. It went on for weeks and at last he called in the local doctor a close friend with whom he sometimes went walking in the nearby hills, something which brought them great pleasure.

After a cursory examination the doctor said, 'Well then I reckon you have a bad case of the cold. It's in both your head and your chest but I think we can fix you up.'

'Och that would be just grand,' replied the minister. 'I am fed up to the back teeth feeling this bad, and this runny nose is a real bother.'

'Aye, aye,' said his friend. 'I reckon all you need is to have a toddy every evening before you go to bed. That should then shift it in a day or so,'

'A toddy!' came the shocked reply, 'that's made with whisky.'

'Well, aye,' the doctor retorted, 'you can make it with brandy or rum if you have a mind to it, but whisky is the best.'

'Och no, no, no, you don't understand,' the minister sounded worried as he said this. 'There has never been a drop of alcohol in this manse in all Janet's time. She would be mortified if she knew I was drinking strong spirits. And you know she talks daily to her four sisters in the village. I wouldn't like to be the subject of gossip about drinking you know.'

'Aha, I see,' mused the doctor. 'But we might have a way round this. I really do think that the toddy would do you good, man.'

'Well, what do you suggest?' asked the reverend McDrouthy.

'Well. I take it you shave of a night?' the doctor queried.

'Well not every night, but two or three times a week, aye,' said McDrouthy.

'All right then, I'll drop by later today with a bottle and you can lock it in your desk. Just ask Janet for some shaving water before you go to bed. Use some of the hot water to make yourself a toddy and shave with the rest and she'll be none the wiser,' explained the doctor.

'Och, that seems a bit underhand,' the minister went on.

'Never mind that, it'll do you good. Now I'm off

but I'll be back later with a bottle,' said the doctor heading for the door.

Sure enough the doctor was back later in the day with in fact a couple of bottles in his big doctor's bag. These he left with the minister and went off on his rounds of the nearby countryside. The following day he was called away to visit a relative who was very ill indeed and didn't come back for almost a month. He had just come back to the village when he ran into Janet outside the Post Office.

'Good day Janet, are you well?' He asked, doffing his hat,

'Och thank you very much doctor I am just as ever I was. Is this you back now?' Came the reply.

'Aye, aye, I'll not be travelling again for a good bit I hope. But tell me Janet, when I left the minister was not too well, is he any better?' He asked.

'Well I suppose you could say that but I think he is coming over strange,' replied the old lady with a wee sigh.

'Yes, yes Janet, what do you mean?' The doctor asked urgently.

'Well he was never a man of vanity, sir, but lately he seems to be thinking a lot more about his appearance,' she replied.

'What exactly do you mean?' He asked.

'Well before he would shave once or twice a week, on a Wednesday and a Saturday, but nowadays he just has to have a shave every night of the week.'

Cave of Raitts

HILE CATTLE RAIDING seems to have been a central function of the Highland tribal warriors from at least the Iron Age, there were those who definitely saw it as a business opportunity. One such opportunity arose in the clever re-use of an ancient monument near Kingussie. This was the Cave of Raitts, an underground structure lined and with boulders and covered with great flat stone slabs. Nobody today knows what such structures were for but hundreds of them have been found all over those parts of Scotland that were occupied by the Picts. The local tradition was that it had been built in one night by a group of giants and giantesses and it was also believed that the roofing slabs had originally come from a nearby standing stone circle, a type of monument that is at least five thousand years old. Whatever the antiquity of the structure, it was put to use by a group of caterans.

They were McNivens, a sept of the Clan Mackintosh who lived in the hills to the south of Inverness. One of them had the bright idea of building a cottage directly over the underground cavity. Once it was built, two old ladies of the clan were installed in the place and the story was circulated that this was an act of charity on the part of McNiven. Nothing could have been further form the truth. It was part of a daring plan to carry out a whole series of raids on the McPhersons who lived in the area. Knowing there was steady market for fresh meat and hides in Inverness, McNiven reckoned that if he could install himself and a group of his clansmen in the cave unknown to the MacPhersons, they would be able to come out at night, lift cattle and head off over the hills towards Inverness. On the way, they would meet with another group of McNivens on their own land who would carry on to Inverness while the original group would head back to the Cave of Raitts under cover of nightfall and be safe in their hiding place before the alarm was raised the following morning.

The plan worked a treat. Night after night, the MacPhersons were losing cattle and their chief was under a great deal of pressure to stop the raiding. The raiders were careful not to slow themselves down by taking large amounts of cattle at once, but were regularly running off with up to twenty or even thirty beasts. This soon began to have a serious economic effect and the McPhersons were becoming ever more concerned. At last, they hatched a plan themselves to find out what was happening. It was clear that whoever was doing the raiding had some base of operation in the area; the hills around had been scoured to see if there were any cateran based in the summer shielings or other locations on the high ground but no trace had been found. Hamish, a young nephew of the chief who had been raised with relatives to the south was chosen to return as a spy. Disguised as a beggar, his job was to go round every house in the area of Kingussie and

Aviemore to try and discover if anything suspicious was going on. It was some job!

After a couple of weeks of this, during which there had been another series of raids, Hamish came to the house at Raitts. He had already passed this way and had been sent packing by the two old ladies who lived there, who clearly did not like strangers. This made him a little suspicious and when he came back the second time, just after night had fallen, and knocked at their door, he complained of severe pains in his side, and pleaded to be able to sleep overnight by their fire. Now the two elderly McNiven ladies were tough customers but like everyone else in the Highlands they had been brought up to extend hospitality and as the young beggar seemed genuinely ill, they consented to let him in and even to let him sleep by their fire. One of the old women went to a large cupboard and opened it asking if he wanted some food. Noticing that the cupboard was full of bannocks, cheese and different kinds of meat, he thanked them and said because of his pains all he wanted to do was go to sleep.

In truth, he was hungry but was playing his part of being ill. He therefore awoke the just before dawn with an absolutely ravenous hunger on him. Lighting a fir taper form the smouldering fire, he walked over to the cupboard in which he had seen the food. He opened it gently, making no noise. It was empty. There was no cheese, no bannocks and no meat. As he stood there he heard the soft murmur of voices. Blowing out his taper, he listened hard. They were men's voices and they seemed to be coming from below his feet. He lay on the ground to listen but the voices grew fainter. So he stood up again and the voices wee stronger. Relighting the taper, he looked closely at the cupboard. It was set into a strong wooden frame and he suddenly realised that it was a door. A door that led to some sort of cave. At that, he heard the women stirring through the room and, quickly blowing out his taper and hiding it beneath his rags, he lay down again before the fire.

As they came in and lit a lamp, he pretended to waken up. They offered him some porridge and again feigning great pain, he thanked them and left the house just as dawn was streaking the sky. Down the path in front of the house he staggered, clutching his side but as soon as he was out of sight behind some trees he straightened up and began to run. In minutes he was at the house of a fellow MacPherson and while he was given something to eat, word was sent to his uncle to come immediately with as many men as he could.

A couple of hours later, the two ladies at Raitts had some more visitors. This time there was no knock on the door. The MacPhersons burst in and the two women were hauled outside. Hamish then went in with his uncle and showed him the cupboard. They pulled and pulled at the cupboard but it had obviously been jammed form the far side. Then they simply piled dry heather in the cupboard, set it alight and went out of the house. Within minutes, the whole wooden structure was alight and flames had spread to the roof. Coughing and spluttering noises could be heard above the crackle of the flames.

Suddenly, as the fire blazed away, the whole cupboard swung open and up rushed half a dozen McNivens, tears streaming form their eyes and their plaids held over their mouths. In the house itself, the smoke wasn't quite as thick but the whole building was now alight. As one, they took their swords in their hands and rushed out calling their battle cry 'Loch Moy'. The MacPhersons were waiting for them in considerable numbers and within minutes the McNivens lay dead as the cottage over the Cave of Raitts sent a great plume of smoke into the sky over Strathspey.

In order to unmask the McNiven plot, young Hamish MacPherson had taken gross advantage of the hospitality of the two old McNiven women. Just as there were rules governing the giving of hospitality, there were rules governing its acceptance. Once you were under someone's roof and they had given, or offered you food, you were duty bound to fight on their behalf. Effectively, for as long as you were under their roof, you were seen as one of their family, with all the obligations that entailed. By this ancient tradition, Hamish was guilty of betraying the McNiven hospitality, but this was of no consequence to the MacPhersons, who were simply glad to put an end to the raiding. However, there is a local tradition that says to this day the descendants of Hamish MacPherson suffer from chronic, untreatable pains in their sides – as a punishment for his breach of the rules of hospitality!

the daft lad

OWN THE YEARS MANY unfortunate inhabitants of the shores of Loch Ness ended up spending time in the prison in Inverness. For long enough the jail was in a four metre square hole inside the main bridge over the river Ness. This dark hole was covered with a grating and was accessed down a flight of stairs and when the prison in the castle was being built it was used again as a temporary lock up. One of its inhabitants in the latter years of its use was one Alan Cameron from Lochaber who was arrested for stealing cattle as late as the second decade of the 19th century. Now Alan was generally thought of as a bit simple and there were those who said that he had been trying to copy the heroes of an old story about the Cateran when he was caught lifting the cattle. Be that as it may Alan was locked up in the old dungeon. As ever in those far off days the welfare of prisoners was never high on the agenda of the local authorities and those who were locked up generally had to rely on their friends or family to feed them. Alan, far from his own people, had no-one to supply him with the necessities of life and depended upon the good graces of the locals. This was however a bit of a mixed blessing as mischievous lads and lasses of the town had a habit of playing a trick on anyone in such straits. They would let down bread on a string through the grating and torment prisoners by pulling and jerking on the string. It was a pretty cruel sport but in the end the miscreant usually ended up with the bread and was grateful for it. In fact so often was this happening that Alan at one point became fed up one day with what was on offer and called out to his persecutors, 'I'll tak nae oat, naethin but the white bannock!' He had become sated with the standard oatmeal bannock or oatcake and preferred to eat white bread which some of the better off children had been tormenting him with. In such ways the palate can be improved. After a while the new jail was complete and Alan was hauled off there.

Now at this time there was a great deal of trouble in the countryside as people were being moved off their ancestral lands to be replaced by sheep in a widespread campaign that has become known as the Highland Clearances. Quite a while before that much of the Lowlands had likewise been cleared of its rural population, but that in no way diminished the hardship that was forced on the Highland people. In many cases throughout the Highland areas the local people had been living on the same land for generations beyond counting but with the old clan ways long gone the lairds, or landlords, saw greater profit in having sheep on the hills rather than people. Often entire communities were turfed out some to live hand-to-mouth on the coast, others to drift into the growing cities of Scotland and England, and many, many more were driven from the land of their birth to countries far over the sea. That so many of them prospered in such places as America, Australia, Canada and New Zealand in no way diminishes the dreadful way they were treated by the landowners of the time, with the full backing of the British government. However the 'progressive' lairds did not get it all their own way and there were riots in many places including Ross-shire. Because the courts were on the side of money and influence and thus against the people many of the rioters ended up being sentenced to prison and so it was that Alan Cameron found himself with a company of Ross-shire men who had tried to defend their homes and families. Having been told when they arrived that Alan was no more than an idiot they paid him little heed. These Highland lads, used to the fresh air and healthy life of the bens and glens, were in no mood to put up with being imprisoned especially as they well understood that the law was being used against them and for the interests of the landowners. If the law was unjust why should they pay it any mind. If they worked together and had help from their relatives outside they were sure they could make their escape and head off on one of the many emigrant ships that were sailing across the Atlantic from the Clyde ports.

So they laid their plans. As they had regular visitors bringing them food, it wasn't too difficult for a few tools to be smuggled in. At last the chosen night came and the Ross-shire lads, over a dozen of them, worked together in total silence to take the door of their prison cell completely off its hinges. Quietly laying it down they moved down the stairs to the ground floor entrance of the prison, unaware that Alan had been watching their every move and was creeping down stairs behind them. The lock on the main gate of the prison proved easy to open with the tools they had and in the dark of the night they slipped out of the prison and away. Just behind them came the Daft Lad they had ignored and he, like them, disappeared in the night. They had friends waiting to help them get clean away. Alan was on his own with only his wits to rely on but, despite what people thought, there was nothing wrong with his wits. He headed back to Lochaber, dug up the money he had hidden and saying goodbye to the few cousins he had in the area, he too went off to Greenock, where he took a ship to North America, and was never seen in Scotland again.

landscape

the CORRYVRECKAN and
the CAILLEACH

NE OF THE MOST spectacular and awe-inspiring sights in nature is a maelstrom or sea whirlpool. These magnificent spinning cauldrons are formed where tides crash or sea water is forced into narrow vortices. There are two particular well-known maelstroms in Europe – the Maelstrom off the Lofoten Islands near the coast of Norway and the gulf of Corryvreckan between Jura and Scarba in the Scottish Inner Hebrides. These magnificent examples of nature in the raw have long held a particular place in the human psyche, and have myths and legends associated with them that seem to come from the edge of time. The Gulf of Corryvreckan is over 300 feet deep but when the whirlpool is at full power the depth of the water is said to be less than a hundred feet. The particular cause of this awesome power is a subterranean spike off the coast of Scarba which causes the great Atlantic waves to form into a giant vortex and create the Corryvreckan whirlpool. It is a dangerous place and local fishermen and sailors have a wealth of stories of its dangers. Even on calm days the swell of the Corryvreckan can be several feet. The spike which causes this massive geophysical event is called An Cailleach, and thereby hangs a tale.

For the Cailleach was the Hag of Winter, a giant creature who controlled the weather and who formed the land of Scotland itself, mountain and glen, loch and river. Stories are told of the Cailleach on many of our great mountains such as Ben Nevis, Ben Wyvis, Schiehallion and place-names commemorating her survive on places as far apart as Lochnagar in Aberdeenshire and Goat Fell on Arran. And here between the isles of Jura and Scarba lies the Corryvreckan, a name which in its oldest Gaelic form *Coire Bhreacan*, means, the Cauldron of the Plaid. The plaid is the ancient one-piece garment of the Highlander and its name *breacan*, means speckled, for is it not the case that the plaids were made of tartan, that multi-coloured cloth that speaks of Scotland across the globe? Well that is true but the plaid of the Cailleach was different. For she was the first born, the oldest living creature on the planet and her plaid was pure white.

And so the story tells us that every year as the end of summer came and the wildness of winter was looming – in olden times, the year was thought of as having but two seasons, summer and winter – the Cailleach would come here to the waters between Jura and Scarba. And here she would wash her plaid in the great cauldron of the Corryvreckan. And as she did this the waters would surge and thunder, the noise being heard as far away as the long isle of Harris and Lewis many miles to the north-west. And this was the time we know the tides ran fiercest causing the great swirling surge of the whirlpool to create a physical cauldron in the sea itself. This happens every year and has done so since the dawn of time. Within living memory fishermen, making sure to keep well clear of the whirlpool as it roared, would whisper of' 'the Old Woman washing her blanket' and would talk of the whirlpool as 'the breath of the goddess under the waves.' And so it was said for years beyond numbering that the Cailleach would take her plaid, now shining white in the first weak sun of winter, and lay it out to dry over Ben Nevis and Mamore Hills. And this it was believed was what gave rise to the first snowfall of winter, year after year after year.

the lost fiddler

HROUGHOUT SCOTLAND there are ancient mounds associated with supernatural creatures. Many of these mounds are actual prehistoric burial mounds that are linked in tradition with the fairies but in the northern isles of Orkney and Shetland they are liked to trowes, or trowies. These are generally malign supernatural creatures, very like the Norse trolls, for the northern isles have long, long cultural links with Scandinavia. Near Papa Stour in Orkney lies Sadness and here there is tale of trowes. A crofter lived here with his children and like the rest of the crofters he got a living from both land and sea. He was poor but kept himself, his wife and bairns fed, clothed and housed. It was a hard but healthy life and he was generally pretty content with his lot. He often entertained his family in the long dark evenings of the Orkney winter with his fiddle playing, for fiddle players have a long tradition in the northern islands. One late afternoon he had headed down to a rocky part of the seashore to fish for sillocks. The fishing was good and he stayed later than he had intended. It began to get dark but he was getting so many fish he tried for one more, several times. At last it was too dark to carry on and he decided to head home. He had a good haul of fish that would keep his family going for a good few days.

It was a dark and moonless night in late autumn,
but there was little cloud and he wasn't worried about
getting back home safely. After all hadn't he known this
land since birth?

Making his way back towards his croft slowly and
carefully he came near a mound he had long ago been
told was home to the trowes. He had never thought too
much about them since he was a lad but as he came
near to the mound he saw a golden light shining out
from it. And he could hear music. Fiddle music.
Fiddle music like he had never heard before. He went
up to the mound and placing his bundle of fish on the
ground he carefully looked round the edge of the door
that the light was coming out of. Strange, he thought,
I've never seen a door here before. But if that was strange
what met his eyes when he looked inside the mound
was very much stranger indeed. The mound was full
of trowes dancing. Now trowes, unlike the fairies,
were not beautiful beings at all but their dancing was
extremely graceful and the music that they were dancing
to seemed to put him in a trance. It was beautiful and
it felt as if it had entered his very heart. He looked and
saw that the creature playing the fiddle was a massive,
gruesome beast, with scaly skin, great tusk-like teeth
and red eyes. It mattered not a bit, the music had him
under its spell and he stepped in to be closer to it. He did
not notice the door closing slowly behind him.

His wife had gone to bed when he wasn't home by
dark and when she awoke she was alone. This had

never happened before. At once she leapt up and ran down to where she thought her man had been the previous night. There was no sign of him. As she came back to their wee house she passed the trowe mound but paid it no heed. Nor did she see the sillocks lying in the grass beside the mound. She was hoping that her man had returned while she was out, but no, there were only the children back at the house. That day she went to her neighbours and told them her man was missing. A search party was put together and they covered every inch of that part of the island. There was no sign of the missing crofter at all. They were all sad and came to the conclusion that he must have either slipped and fell into the sea, knocking his head on a rock and drowning. Or, some others said, a freak wave may well have come up on that still night and carried him off. It wouldn't be the first time. Others though, quietly, in their own homes talked of the possibility that he had been stolen away by the trowes. No one would say that in public though.

Life became harder for his family but his wife struggled on, and with help from her neighbours managed to keep the wee croft going and her children grew up healthy and well-fed, if even poorer than they had been before. As they came into adulthood, the sadness of the place that had come upon them when their father disappeared had its effect. One after another the five of them moved away to Kirkwall and Stromness where they wouldn't have to face the daily reminders of the great sadness of their lives. In time too the mother went to live with one of her sons in the town, and the croft passed into other hands.

One autumn night the grandfather of the family who lived in the croft was sitting gazing into the fire. Around him were his son, his wife and half a dozen bonny grandchildren all waiting for what they knew was to come. Grandfather would tell the stories, old stories of heroes and battles, silkies and trowes, before they would go to their beds. The grandfather had lived in the house since he had been born and loved the place dearly. The night was a bit wild and the wind was getting up a good blow outside. Suddenly the door of the cottage opened and the wind blew in. They all looked up. There, framed in the doorway was a man dressed in rags and clutching a strange looking fiddle the like of which none of them had seen before. The man was old and had a puzzled look on his face. The children ready to hear tales of the olden times laughed in surprise, the eldest, Robert looking keenly at the weird fiddle in the man's hands. He was learning the fiddle himself but this one seemed a strange shape and appeared to have extra strings. He couldn't figure it out at all.

Then the stranger spoke, 'What are you all doing here in my house?'

The mother of the children looked sharply at her man. Who was this strange man? Was he right in the head? He caught her meaning and stood up. The man spoke again.

'I said what are you doing in my house?' and this time there was a note of something like fear in his voice.

The old man by the fire signalled to his son to sit down and said to the stranger, 'We'll get to that in a bit, but it's a wild night out there. Close the door and come warm yourself by the fire, my friend.'

Looking nervously around at the children and the cottage he closed the door and came to the fire. He sat down and looking around repeated that this was his home. Then he said 'Where are my children? Where is my Maggie?' All the time looking around in confusion.

The grandfather looked at him and asked gently, 'What is your name?'

'What?' the man said. 'My name? My name is Andrew Fimister and this is my house.'

'Andrew Fimister, Andrew Fimister,' he murmured. 'I know the name. Ah I remember, my grandfather told me there was a family here before he came. They were called Fimister. He told me that the man of the house went missing one evening, and it was around this time of year.'

The stranger looked at him, his eyes growing large in his head.

'When was this? When?' He gasped.

'Oh it would be about a hundred years ago now I think," said the grandfather looking keenly at the white-haired stranger.

'A hundred years. A hundred years,' the man whispered, 'And what of my wife and my bonny bairns?'

'Well they say they all moved off to Kirkwall and Stromness, but that was a century ago, they will all be long gone now.'

'Gone. All gone,' the stranger mumbled to himself and they could all see the tears running down his old, lined face. 'My bonny bairns and my Maggie all gone.'

He fell silent and sat looking into the fore for what seemed a long time. Nobody spoke. Then the stranger seemed to shiver and looked directly at the grandfather.

'I see it now,' he said and nodded. 'I thank you sir, it is time I too went.'

And saying this, he got up, still clutching his fiddle and went out of the door gently closing it behind him.

The children all looked at each other, struck dumb with surprise.

'We had best let him be, I think,' said the grandfather. 'The poor man has been with the trowes all this time.'

And they all sat quietly, thinking their own thoughts. Well, not quite all. Robert went into another room and quietly climbed out of the window. He wanted to see what would happen to the stranger. And the fiddle.

He watched as the man walked down to the foot of the cottage garden. The wind had dropped, the sky had cleared and high above crossing the sky there were faint traces of the Fairy Dancers, the Northern Lights that generally came later in the wintertime.

And Robert watched as the strange old man stood there and raised the fiddle to his chin. He stood and listened as Fimister played a tune on the old instrument.

It was a tune he had never heard before, but that he would never forget. The man finished the tune. Then he started it again. Robert listened as he had never listened before. This time as he finished the old fiddler dropped the fiddle, and as the young lad watched, fell to the ground. Robert ran forward. There on the ground was nothing but a heap of rags and a skeleton that before his eyes was turning to dust. Beside it lay the old fiddle and as Robert reached forward to pick it up it too turned to dust. Just then the wind picked up and scattered the dust of man and fiddle across the land. But Robert never ever forgot that tune and in time became known through all of Orkney as the fiddler who played the Trowe's tune.

wildlife

conachar's dog

NOTHER WEEL-KENNT local tale concerned a favourite hound of the great warrior Conochar. It was known as *An Cu Mor*, the Big Dog and was of an extraordinary size. In its prime, coursing through the mountains and glens with his master hunting deer and wild boar, there was no dog anywhere that was a match for *An Cu Mor*. Its great size and strength was matched by its speed and intelligence. For many years it was a faithful companion to Big Conochar as he hunted the hills around Loch Ness. But all things must pass and when the time came that age came on him, *An Cu Mor* was no longer the magnificent beast he once was. His hair grew grey and strength began to fail him. So another hunting dog took his place at Conochar's side and *An Cu Mor* went less and less from the site of Castle Urquhart till at last he never went beyond the wooden walls of the fort overlooking the great loch. Although it saddened him Conochar decided that it was time that *An Cu Mor* should be put down. Although it had been his faithful companion for many years, it was of no use to him and though this saddened him there was nothing he could do about the passing of time. It seemed that the dog itself too was saddened at the passing of its former powers and just lay around listlessly near to the fire, day after day.

Maybe watching the once-proud animal, lazing by the fire, when it used to course the hills for days on end, reminded Conochar of his own mortality, we can never know, but one day he decided it was time to be rid of *An Cu Mor*.

He told those around him of his intention but Beathag, one of the old women of the community said 'Naw, Naw Conochar. Let the dog live, his own day awaits him and it is not yet.'

Like all men of his time Conochar knew it was usually a good move to listen to the words of old women. They had seen and learned much in their long lives and their wisdom and understanding were known to be of great use to the community. Also, as Conochar well knew, many of them had great knowledge of plant and herb lore, handed down over centuries, and some of them even had ways of understanding the future. So it was always a good idea to pay attention to what the old women said.

Anyway that summer a great boar had been seen in the hills to the north-west of Urquhart and every man who went out to hunt for it had failed to come back. Their fearsomely mangled bodies were found high in the hills and it seemed as if this boar was beyond the skill and power of any man to hunt it down and kill it. Soon it began to be seen close to Urquhart itself and the women began to fear that it could come close enough to attack the children. Something had to be done and, as the chief, Conochar knew it was up to him.

So he readied himself to go after the great boar.

One morning he arose just after dawn, picked three good spears, strapped his shield to his back, belted his sword around his waist and set off to the woods. He had intended taking his current favourite hound with him but when he stepped outside who was frisking about like a puppy but *An Cu Mor*. It seemed as if the years had disappeared from him overnight. Excitedly he ran up to his master and started to lick his hand,

'Woah, boy, easy there now,' said Conochar with a smile, for the sight of the life in the old dog made him happy. 'Ah you want to come along with me on the hunt do you?'

By now the dog was leaping up and then falling to its feet, spinning round and leaping up to try and lick its master again and again.

Conochar was warmed to his heart as he remembered all the years this fine old hound had worked with him hunting in the hills and he said, 'Fine, fine *An Cu Mor*, you can come with me this day, but be warned it is a fearsome beast we are after, and neither of us may return from such a hunt.' As he said this he patted the excited dog on the head and this seemed to calm the creature down a little.

Still as they headed off into the forest the dog scampered around him like a puppy, and the sight made Conochar smile. Soon they were deep in the hills. Reports that the great beast was getting ever nearer to Urquhart were proved right when within the hour Conochar, turned a corner in a wee glen he knew well, where the trees

formed a dark, cool tunnel on the hottest of days, and
there before him was the boar. It was half as big again as
any he had ever seen before and he barely had time to
ready himself when the beast attacked. The force of its
charge splintered the spear that Conochar had braced
against a handy rock, but as the great beast tore at him
An Cu Mor lunged at it and grabbed its rear right leg.

Squealing with pain the boar turned from Conochar
to try and gore the courageous dog with its tusks.
The two animals spun round and round as Conochar
got another spear ready and as the boar shook *An Cu
Mor* off, he lunged with his spear. Using all his strength
he could barely pierce the skin of the monstrous animal
and back it turned toward him. As it rushed him again,
An Cu Mor once more leapt at the animal and clamped
its teeth into its left rear leg. The beast's charge splintered
Conochar's second spear and he was thrown up into the
air to fall onto the rocks, winded. As he lay gasping for
breath *An Cu Mor* attacked the boar with even greater
ferocity. By now the noble dog was covered in blood
from wounds caused by the boar's tusks. Despite the
blood loss *An Cu Mor's* courage never flinched. The wild
boar came at it again and flipped it up in the air
attempting to catch the dog on its tusks but missing.
The dog rolled over and over and the boar closed in.
Conochar had managed to regain his breath and taking
his last spear ran once more at the beast as it closed in on
the severely wounded hound. The poor dog was snarling
as the boar attacked but its right rear leg was folded under

it and it could not get out of the way of the charge. Just as
the great beast was about to thunder into the dog,
Conochar threw himself at it with his spear in both hands.
This time the point of the spear went clean through the
tough, hairy skin of the great pig. It let out a dreadful roar
and swung back towards the man ripping the spear from
his hands. Conochar rolled away and leapt to his feet,
drawing his sword as he did so. The animal stood
opposite him, only a few feet away, the spear sticking out
from its side. Conochar could clearly see that the whole of
the spear head and about two hands of the shaft had gone
into the creature's body. It was growling with pain as its
red eyes focused on the human before it. Again it rushed.
This time however was different. The spear had bit deep
into its body and some of the ferocity had gone. Conochar
realised that it had slowed down as he jumped to his left
and brought his sword down on the creature's great skull.
There was a terrible crack and the creature sprawled to
the ground sliding forward against a rock as its legs gave
way. But it wasn't finished yet. Just as Conochar got ready
to deliver another blow the beast whipped round and rose
to its feet. It was breathing heavily and a great gush of
blood came from the spear wound in its side. It let out a
terrible roar and came again at Conochar. Somehow it
seemed to have regained its strength and Conochar was
bowled over after taking a deep gash to his left leg. The
beast skidded by and turned again. Conochar couldn't get
to his feet. The blow had given him a dead leg! The beast
took in great gulps if air as it stared directly at its foe,

getting ready for the final charge. Conochar struggled to his feet and then he saw a wondrous thing.

Completely silently, although dripping blood and in dreadful pain. *An Cu Mor* was creeping up behind the boar, dragging its useless left leg behind it. Just as the beast pawed the ground to surge forward again and finish off this two-legged pest, the brave dog sank its teeth into the beast's back left leg again. This time the dog refused to let go, The boar whirled, *An Cu Mor* was thrown up in the air but held on. Round and round the two animals turned rolling over on each other, the boar trying to gore the old dog. Once, twice, three times it managed to pierce the faithful hound's skin, but it did not let go. Conochar by now had managed to get to his feet. Ignoring the blood dripping from his leg he inched his way towards the whirling animals. Just as he got close *An Cu Mor's* strength gave out and it let go of the boar's leg. The creature closed in for the kill. It did not even sense the man behind it as it focused on this four legged pest that had given it such pain. It did not hear the sound of Conochar's great sword as he brought it down with all his remaining strength on its head. Straight through the bone and into the brain the blade went. The boar dropped like a stone, dead at Conochar's feet the sword stuck in its great skull. Conochar too fell, across the great hairy body of the slain boar. After a few minutes he managed to pull himself off the beast's body and crawl to *An Cu Mor*. He held the great dog in his arms as it looked up at him, clearly breathing its last.

Its body was torn to shreds but no sound of pain came from the noble beast. As its life slowly ebbed, the creature looked into its master's eyes, faithful to the very last.

In later years Conochar would tell the story of his faithful dog's final service and he always finished with these words, 'He was the finest hound any man ever had and as he passed on from this life to the next, what I saw in his eyes was pride. There will never be another dog like him.' And often as he himself aged, he would sit in his great fort on the shore of the loch, fingering the scars he got in the battle with the great boar, and thinking fondly on the dog who certainly had his day.

a kelpie tale

HE CONAN IS AS bonny a river as we have in the north country. But its bonny wooded banks are places for enjoying the day in—not for passing the night. It's not one of the great rivers that come thundering down over rapids or swirls in great deep pools, it's a kind of gentler stream yet it has far more than it's share of dark takes. There's hardly half a mile of it that doesn't have some kind of story of the kelpie or other water-spirits, and in truth many people have drowned in the Conan over the years. It's an unsettling river right enough.

One of these stores took place not far from Conan House itself. There's a sort of swampy meadow that the river runs through, and in the middle of it there's a wee knoll, covered with willows and looking just like an island. On it there is an old burying-ground and the tumbled down ruins of an old, old church. Hundreds of years old, though it was still in use a couple of centuries back. And that's an eerie spot too I can tell you. On this stretch of the river the woods press down on each side, dark and gloomy but back when the church was still in use the area was clear and crops were being grown. One bonnie autumn day a bunch of local lads were busy bringing in the crops around noon when suddenly they heard a great booming voice, 'The hour but not the man has come.'

They all turned at the sound and there close by
the old church, in the river at the spot that they called
the false ford, was a kelpie, a bonnie big black horse,
with a silver harness and a gold saddle on its back.
At that spot the river looks like it has shallowed out
because of a ripple on the water but it is a treacherous
spot. And as they watched the kelpie repeated itself,
'The hour but not the man has come.' Then it shook its
mane and dived below the water into the deep pool just
upriver from where it had appeared.

Now the lads were a bit upset at this as you can
imagine and as they were all standing around looking
at each other and wondering what to say they heard
a sound. It was the sound of hoof beats. It was coming
from up above them, on the hill slope to the south.
There was a man on horseback going hell-for-leather.
And he was heading straight for the false ford. Suddenly
they understood what was going to happen and four of
the youngest lads ran straight towards the approaching
horseman.

They managed to get him to pull up and told him
what they had just seen. He was obviously in a hurry
and looking around said, 'That's just silly superstition.
Let me pass. I must be on my way now.'

But the lads knew what they had seen and were
not going to let him pass. In fact they had to pull him
from his horse to stop him going on. They manhandled
him and took him to the church where they put him
inside and secured the door to stop him getting out,

leaving his horse back in the field. They were sure that if they could just keep him safe until the hour was up, he would be safe from the evil beast and he could be on his way. So after the hour was up they came and opened the door. They shouted to the stranger to come out, but answer came there none. So they went in. There at the far end of the old church was the stranger stooped over the font. They ran to him to find his body cold and lifeless his head in three inches of water in the font. Nobody much goes there now but if you do you can still see the old font in the ruins. And it just shows the power of the kelpie, nothing the men could do could alter its dreadful prophecy.

COLUMBA AND NESSIE

OWEVER IT WASN'T only deer that Columba ran into when in the area around Loch Ness. Another time he was on his way to Inverness and he and his companions were trying to find a way across the deep waters of the loch when they came across a group of people near the shores who were busy burying the body of a young man. As they stood and watched the proceedings, one of Columba's monks, who spoke Pictish, asked a bystander how the young lad had died. He listened a while then turned to Columba and informed the saint that the poor youth had been swimming in the loch when a gigantic snake-like creature had come up from the depths and taken a great bite out of his side. The lad had just managed to swim to the shore before he died.

Columba was busy looking over the loch as the monk spoke. Spotting a small boat on the far side, he said to the monk, 'Look over yonder. There is a boat that could carry us over the waters of this loch. Just you swim over and row it back over to us.'

The monk looked long and hard at the saint. Had he been listening? Didn't he understand about the ominous creature in the water? However he knew that Columba had power over many things including the weather and almost every creature on the planet. So with total faith in his leader, he took off his robe and waded out into the cold waters of the loch. He was only a few yards out into the loch swimming towards the boat, when a hundred yards ahead of him the head of a monstrous eel-like creature broke the surface of the water. At once it headed towards the swimming man. The funeral party saw what was happening and many of them began to yell and point. Others fell to their knees and wept. Even some of Columba's monks fell to their knees and they began to implore the Lord to save their friends from this dreadful monster. The great scaly creature bore down on the young monk, as Columba calmly watched. Then just as the evil-looking creature seemed about to strike, he formed the shape of the cross in the air with his right hand and called out in his powerful voice, 'Go no further here, nor touch the man. Turn now, turn and go back whence you came!'

The creature which had reared up to strike at the swimming monk, seemed to stop absolutely still in the water. It was as if it had been pierced by a spear. The upper half of its slimy and scaly body stood straight out of the water and its greats ugly head turned to look at the saint. To those watching it seemed that the great monster hung in the air forever before it shook its head, let out a high-pitched squeal, then turned and dived back below the waves of Loch Ness. At a sign from Columba the monk, who had been treading water as the foul beast had approached, continued swimming to the other side and fetched the boat back. Soon the saint and his companions were over the loch and carried peacefully on their way towards Inverness. And nothing more was seen of the monstrous beast. Well not until well over a thousand years later, though nowadays we call her Nessie.

Share, explore, experience and celebrate our storytelling heritage.

0131 556 9579

The **Scottish Storytelling Centre** is the home of Scotland's stories on Edinburgh's picturesque Royal Mile. The Centre presents a seasonal programme of storytelling, theatre, dance, music and literature, supported by exciting visual arts, craft and multimedia exhibitions. The Centre also hosts the **Scottish International Storytelling Festival** in October, which is a highlight of Scotland's autumn.

You've seen the landscape, vibrant cities and historic buildings, now experience the magic of live stories and feed your imagination. Don't miss out on the warmth and energy of modern culture inspired by tradition!

www.scottishstorytellingcentre.co.uk

Some other books published by **LUATH** PRESS

On the Trail of Scotland's Myths and Legends

Stuart McHardy

ISBN 978-1-84282-049-0 PBK £7.99

 Mythical animals, supernatural beings, heroes, giants and goddesses come alive and walk Scotland's rich landscape as they did in the time of the Scots, Gaelic and Norse bards of the past.

Visiting over 170 sites across Scotland, Stuart McHardy traces the lore of our ancestors, connecting ancient beliefs with traditions still alive today. Presenting a new picture of who the Scots are and where they have come from, this book provides an insight into a unique tradition of myth, legend and folklore that has marked the language and landscape of Scotland.

Tales of Bonnie Prince Charlie and the Jacobites

Stuart McHardy

ISBN: 978-1-908373-23-6 PBK £7.99

 Great battles, great characters and great stories underpin our understanding of the Jacobite period; one of the most romanticised eras in Scottish History.

From the exploits of charismatic Bonnie Prince Charlie to the many ingenious ways the Jacobites out-witted the Redcoats, Stuart McHardy has gathered together some of the best tales from the period. Find out the best way to escape from Edinburgh Castle and where to look for Prince Charlie's enchanted gold. Discover the story behind one Highlander who swapped his kilt for a dress, and more, in this salute to the ancient Scots tradition of storytelling.

Luath Storyteller: Tales of the Picts

Stuart McHardy

ISBN 978-1-84282-097-1 PBK £5.99

 For many centuries the people of Scotland have told stories of their ancestors, a mysterious tribe called the Picts. This ancient Celtic-speaking people, who fought off the might of the Roman Empire, are perhaps best known for their Symbol Stones – images carved into standing stones left scattered across Scotland, many of which have their own stories. Here for the first time these tales are gathered together with folk memories of bloody battles, chronicles of warriors and priestesses, saints and supernatural beings. From Shetland to the Border with England, these ancient memories of Scotland's original inhabitants have flourished since the nation's earliest days and now are told afresh, shedding new light on our ancient past.

Luath Storyteller: Tales of Edinburgh Castle

Stuart McHardy

ISBN 978-1-905222-95-7 PBK £5.99

 Who was the new-born baby found buried inside the castle walls?

Who sat down to the fateful Black Dinner?

Who was the last prisoner to be held in the dungeons, and what was his crime?

Towering above Edinburgh, on the core of an extinct volcano, sits a grand and forbidding fortress. Edinburgh Castle is one of Scotland's most awe-inspiring and iconic landmarks. A site of human habitation since the Bronze Age, the ever-evolving structure has a rich and varied history and has been of crucial significance, militarily and strategically, for many hundreds of years.

Tales of Edinburgh Castle is a salute to the ancient tradition of storytelling and paints a vivid picture of the castle in bygone times, the rich and varied characters to whom it owes its notoriety, and its central role in Scotland's history and identity.

Luath Storyteller: Tales of Loch Ness

Stuart McHardy

ISBN 978-1-906307-59-2 PBK £5.99

 We all know the Loch Ness Monster. Not personally, but we've definitely heard of it. Stuart McHardy knows a lot more stories about Loch Ness monsters, fairies and heroes than most folk, and he has more than a nodding acquaintance with Nessie, too.

From the lassie whose forgetfulness created the loch to St Columba's encounter with a rather familiar sea-monster nearly 1,500 years ago, from saints to hags to the terrible *each-uisge*, the waterhorse that carries unwitting riders away to drown and be eaten beneath the waters of the loch, these tales are by turns funny, enchanting, gruesome and cautionary. Derived from both history and legends, passed by word of mouth for untold generations, they give a glimpse of the romance and glamour, the danger and the magic of Scotland's Great Glen.

Story provided the children of the ancient tribes with their education, their self-awareness and their understanding of the world they inhabited.
STUART McHARDY

Luath Storyteller: Tales of Whisky

Stuart McHardy

ISBN 978-1-906817-41-1 PBK £5.99

 The truth is of course that whisky was invented for a single, practical reason – to offset Scotland's weather.

Raise your glasses and toast this collection of delightful tales, all inspired by Scotland's finest achievement: whisky. We see how the amber nectar can help get rid of a pesky giant, why should never build a house without offering the foundations a dram and how it can bring a man back from the brink of death.

Whisky has a long and colourful history in Scotland, causing riots and easing feuds, and McHardy has gathered together stories which have been passed down through many generations, often over a wee nip. *Tales of Whisky* is a tribute to the Scottish sense of humour and love of fine storytelling.

Luath Press Limited
committed to publishing well written books worth reading

LUATH PRESS takes its name from Robert Burns, whose little collie Luath (*Gael.*, swift or nimble) tripped up Jean Armour at a wedding and gave him the chance to speak to the woman who was to be his wife and the abiding love of his life. Burns called one of 'The Twa Dogs' Luath after Cuchullin's hunting dog in Ossian's *Fingal*. Luath Press was established in 1981 in the heart of Burns country, and is now based a few steps up the road from Burns' first lodgings on Edinburgh's Royal Mile.

Luath offers you distinctive writing with a hint of unexpected pleasures.

Most bookshops in the UK, the US, Canada, Australia, New Zealand and parts of Europe either carry our books in stock or can order them for you. To order direct from us, please send a £sterling cheque, postal order, international money order or your credit card details (number, address of cardholder and expiry date) to us at the address below. Please add post and packing as follows: UK – £1.00 per delivery address; overseas surface mail – £2.50 per delivery address; overseas airmail – £3.50 for the first book to each delivery address, plus £1.00 for each additional book by airmail to the same address. If your order is a gift, we will happily enclose your card or message at no extra charge.

Luath Press Limited
543/2 Castlehill
The Royal Mile
Edinburgh EH1 2ND
Scotland
Telephone: 0131 225 4326 (24 hours)
Fax: 0131 225 4324
email: sales@luath.co.uk
Website: www.luath.co.uk